SWEATER WEATHER

Sapphire Falls Orchard
Book 1

SHANNON O'CONNOR

Cover by *conceptsbycanea*.

Edited & Proofread by Victoria Ellis of *Cruel Ink Editing & Design*.

Formatted by Shannon O'Connor.

❀ Formatted with Vellum

Content Warnings

Please note some of these might be considered spoilers for parts of the story.

- Negative coming out experience/non supportive parents
Past experiences, not on page

- Recreational Marijuana/Marijuana Edibles use
on page representation

- Death of a character
on page representation, death happens before book starts
- Mentions of Character terminal illness
Past experiences, not on page

For every fall lover, looking for something more gay.

Sweater Weather
Playlist

Sweater Weather - The Neighbourhood

pretty - JVKE

Fire and the Flood - Vance Joy

Too Sweet - Hozier

Lovefool - The Cardigans

Supermassive Black Hole - Muse

a thousand years - Christina Perri

always been you - lovelytheband

Shameless - Camila Cabello

I Hate Myself for Loving You - Joan Jett & the Blackhearts

True Love - P!nk ft. Lily Allen

Dirty Thoughts - Chloe Adams

Iris - mgk & Julia Wolf

Electric Love - BORNS

Oceans - Seafret

Mad - Renee Rapp

u turn me on (but u give me depression) - LOLO

I Wanna Be The One You Call - Benson Boone

we fell in love in October - girl in red

this is what autumn feels like - JVKE

ONE

Bells

I taste the last sip of a latte I grabbed in Grand Central, and the second I step into this small town, I know it might be the last good coffee I'll get. Tossing the cup in the clean garbage can, I realize I'm not in Kansas anymore. I roll my suitcase down the stairs and stop to look around for a cab. I know better than to attempt to find an Uber here. I don't even know if the app works in this town. There's one single black cab, the driver standing outside the car smoking a cigarette on the hood.

"Can I get a ride?" I ask, rolling my suitcase toward them.

They flick the cigarette to the side and look me over. An uneasy feeling flies over me as they look from my heels to my copper hair. "Cash only, and I don't take music requests."

"Fine by me." I shrug.

He nods and takes my suitcase, popping the trunk behind him. I tell him where I'm staying—one of my family's apartments right in town. It isn't too far to walk, but I refuse to mess up my heels by walking on this uneven ground. Aren't small towns supposed to be better at town upkeep or something? I appreciate that he doesn't try to make small talk, and the ride is quick. I hand him an extra twenty, and he carries my suitcase to the front door.

My parents are staying at the hotel just outside of town, but I asked to stay here. I didn't want to be under the same roof as my parents, and they own a lot of property in this town. They won't be in the same room together—they haven't shared a room in years. Plopping my bag on the floor, I collapse on the bed. My heels fall off, and I sigh. I'm not tired enough for bed, but I need to do something to take the edge off. I'm stressed enough about seeing my entire extended family tomorrow.

I decide to look up the closest bar, which is apparently less than a three-minute walk. I hook my sweater around my shoulders, check my makeup, and put my heels back on. It's mid-May, but the weather is surprisingly chilly.

Once I reach the bar, I take note of the rusty signage. The lights are on inside, so it must be open—that's what matters. I sit down at the bar and wait for the bartender to notice me. I'm used to being ignored in bars; I'm plus-sized, and that means, for some reason, that I'm invisible. I often melt into the background of life.

I take out a twenty and wave it in the air, knowing money is the way to get attention no matter what you look like or where you are. Sure enough, the broody bartender notices me and walks over with a top-shelf smile.

"What can I get for you?" He'd probably be attractive—if I liked men.

"A dirty martini please—extra olives." I'm really in the mood for some wine, but I have a feeling the only wine they carry in this place comes in a box.

"Coming right up." He makes my drink, and I hand him the twenty, telling him to keep the change.

As I sip my drink, taking the olives out with a toothpick, I look around the place. It seems like a popular spot for a random Wednesday night. It isn't crowded by any means, but it *is* busy. Seems like mostly older men, wearing work jeans and baseball caps with dirt under their fingernails. I'd secretly been hoping to see someone who might take the edge off, but since the crowd is mostly men…

Sigh.

In the morning, I need to get to the funeral home and greet people who probably knew my aunt better than me. My family is all about appearances, and I doubt I'll get away with bailing. I'll put on a brave face and smile my way through it—until the weekend is over. I'm more worried about seeing my parents and having them ask me about work. I'm up for a promotion, and any day now, I'll know if the new title is mine—or if my ex gets the job I've been hoping for. I'm more deserving, but life is often an old boys' club, so I won't be surprised if I'm passed up—again. But I didn't want to face my parents' disappointment over it.

The more pressure they put on me, the more anxious I feel. It isn't like I can tell them I'll be fine if I don't get the promotion; they want to see me constantly social climbing. Just like they did. Now they have multiple houses, millions of dollars they'll never spend…and they're still as unhappy as they were when they had nothing.

"Another round, Bill," a woman says, breaking through my thoughts.

She has slicked back blonde hair, a sharp jawline, and piercing blue eyes. She's thin, but her build is muscular—like she spends a lot of time at the gym. I can see her arms through the red flannel she's wearing. Who is this woman?

"Hey, I'm sorry again—" Bill starts, but the woman holds up a hand.

"Don't mention it," she says firmly.

I'm intrigued by this mystery woman, so just as she's about to head back to her friends, I move my purse—which causes her to bump into my drink. It splatters across the floor, and her eyes meet mine in a panic.

She's right where I want her.

"I'm so sorry!" we both say at the same time.

"I should've looked before moving," I add.

"No, I'm sorry. I didn't realize I was so close." She frowns.

"Don't worry, I got it," Bill says, already walking around the bar.

"Can I make it up to you?" she asks with a slight smile.

"Maybe buy me a drink?" I bat my dark eyelashes at her, hoping my gaydar is working correctly tonight.

"Sure, let me get these to my friends, and I'll be right back." She disappears and is back moments later, asking Bill for two drinks—one for her and one for me.

She slides onto the stool next to me, and I take in her muscular hands. Am I weird for being attracted to hands? Is that a lesbian thing, or do straight people love hands too? Her fingernails are short and clean, but it's the veins running across the backs of her hands that get me. She grips her beer can, and my brain immediately wonders what else she could do with those hands. It's been way too long since I've gotten laid.

"You don't seem like a local. I definitely would've noticed you before," she says with a wink.

"I'm just here for the weekend, hoping to blow off some steam." I twirl my fingers around the stem of my martini glass.

"I think I might be able to help with that. Do you have a name?"

I open my mouth to tell her but stop myself. It's a small town, and chances are my aunt is well known here. The last thing I want is for someone to recognize me and ruin my chances of getting laid tonight.

"What if we don't exchange names?"

"You on the run or something?" She chuckles.

"I just don't plan on being here long," I say with a shrug.

"All right, well I have to call you something. How about City Girl?" Now she's the one batting her eyelashes.

"What will I call you?"

"How about Mac?"

"Sure, that's cute." I laugh.

"What do you say we get out of here?"

"I'm staying a few minutes away. Wanna come over?" I ask, finishing my drink.

"Yeah. Let me just tell my friends, and I'll meet you outside."

She tips back the last of her beer while I gather my things.

Outside, it's gotten darker, the night air cooler. I pull my sweater off my shoulders and actually put it on this time. Part of me wishes I'd taken a shower before coming out, but I'm not gross or anything. A moment later, Mac—yes, that's what I'm calling her now—steps outside, looking even hotter in the moonlight. Is that cliché? Probably. But I'm a little tipsy and she really is beautiful.

"Ready, City Girl?" she asks, smiling, her perfectly white teeth dazzling me.

"Y-yes." I nod.

Mac stills, stepping closer until we're only inches apart. She presses a hand to my cheek, and I freeze at the sudden intimacy of her touch. I don't know why I'm suddenly so nervous. It's not like I've never had a one-night stand before. But when Mac leans in to kiss me, everything shifts.

Her lips touch mine, and my body moves toward hers like a magnet. We're kissing, her hands tangling in my hair while mine wrap around her neck. It feels like we've kissed a million times before.

Familiarity washes over me as her tongue slips into my mouth. I know I won't forget this hookup—hell, I'm suddenly sure I never could. She pulls back and takes my hand.

"I always kiss a woman before bringing her home—or, in this case, going home with her," Mac says, blushing.

I clear my throat. "Why?"

"Because the kiss usually tells you how good everything is going to be."

"Oh yeah? Then how's everything else going to be?" I ask, teasing her with a raised eyebrow.

"Amazing. I have a feeling it's going to be hard to leave your bed."

She's such a smooth talker I almost believe her—but I've heard my fair share of one-liners meant to get someone into bed.

"I guess we should go find out." I wink, and she laces her fingers with mine.

"You lead the way."

Though honestly, I bet she could find my place in a heartbeat if I just gave her the address.

TWO

Tilly

"I thought you said you weren't from town?" I raise an eyebrow as I look around the furnished apartment. I had sort of assumed she was staying with someone—or at the local motel.

"It belongs to my family," she says, kicking off her heels. Part of me wishes she kept them on; I wouldn't mind seeing them over my shoulder. I kick off my Doc Martens and follow City Girl inside.

I have to admit, the *no names* thing is different, but it isn't bad. Right now, everyone in town knows I'm grieving, and it's nice to escape that for a bit. My friends know I have a habit of seducing the tourists, so they won't be worried. One of the only good things about being in a touristy town are the women who pop in from time to time. Most of them wear Chanel perfume, carry Coach bags on their arms, and wear heels that make them taller than me. Not that I need a butch to match me—I love all women—but that nose-in-the-air nonsense? I can't handle it. So far, City Girl seems okay in that department.

"Mac?" I realize I've been dazed for a few moments, because I missed the last thing she said. I'm not drunk or anything, just happily tipsy.

7

"Sorry, I missed that. What did you say?"

"I asked if you want the lights on or off," she says with a laugh. She's taken off her cheetah print sweater, and she's next to the light switch.

"Oh, whatever you want." I shrug. The streetlight pours in through the window, and when she turns the lights off, it creates a surprisingly intimate glow.

I slip my flannel off and toss it onto the chair next to the bed. City Girl unzips her pencil skirt, letting it fall to her feet before stepping over it and placing it on the chair. She slides off her blouse as I take off my jeans. My eyes are on her breasts, perched perfectly in a lace bra that looks uncomfortable as hell, but God what it does to me. Her curves are only highlighted with this lighting. God, she's fucking sexy as hell. She walks over to the bed, and I slide off my black T-shirt, climbing onto the bed next to her.

"Why do I get the feeling I'll need a safe word with you?" she jokes.

"You can have one, City Girl." I smirk.

"Just stay away from my ass, and we're good."

"Same here." I nod.

She pushes me onto the bed and climbs on top of me. She hovers, like she's afraid of me or something, and I pull her body down onto mine. Her soft skin melts into me, her lips crashing into mine. Her cool hands find a home at my waist, and I can't keep mine still—I need to touch every inch of her.

She sucks gently on my lip, and I moan into her mouth. My hands slip around her back, unhooking her bra in record time. She stops kissing me just long enough to sit up, toss it aside, and lean back down to kiss me again.

She kicks my knees apart and slides her thick thigh between my hips. I groan.

"Fuck," I grumble.

Her thigh presses right against my clit through my boxers, sending a pulse through me that makes my whole body shiver.

I reach for her breasts—full, soft, spilling out of my hands—and lean up to take a nipple in my mouth. I tug with my teeth, and she gasps, tossing her head back in pleasure. Her hips buck as my other hand finds her other nipple, pinching until she's whimpering.

Her hand slips between us, and her fingertips brush against my core.

"I think you're wearing too much, Mac," she whispers in my ear.

I nod, breathless.

She slides off me, and I stand to strip the rest of my clothes while she peels off her wet panties and tosses them across the room.

Fuck. Her pussy is so pink, so wet she's dripping.

I climb back onto the bed, kneeling between her legs. She scoots down toward me, and I spread her open with my hand. She's perfectly waxed except for a neat little landing strip.

I lean in and lick her, and her hips jerk toward my face.

A groan rips out of me as I taste her—wet, sweet, perfect. She hooks her legs over my shoulders, her thighs clenching as I suck her clit.

"Oh, shit!" she cries, her thighs tightening around my head.

God, I love fucking women. Not that I know any different—but how does everyone not want to do this?

I'm ravenous, my own pussy dripping as I eat her out. Her whimpers and moans are a song I want to memorize. She toys with her breasts, rolling her nipples between her fingers. I struggle to keep my eyes open, rubbing my thighs together for a little friction.

I slide two fingers inside her, and her eyes fly open. She sits up to watch me, one hand fisting the sheets, the other pushing my head closer to her clit. I suck harder and pump my fingers in and out of her tight heat. Her auburn curls cascade around her shoulders, reminding me of falling autumn leaves.

After a while, my jaw aches, but I don't want to stop if she's close. The problem is, she's been hovering on the edge since I started.

As if reading my mind, she murmurs, "It's hard to make me finish, but if you're tired, you can stop. That felt amazing."

I nod, climbing off my knees. I'm not twenty anymore, and my thighs are going to hate me tomorrow.

"You don't always finish?" I ask.

"Not with a partner, usually." She shrugs like it's no big deal.

"That's not going to stop me from trying." I wink, and she blushes.

"Would you sit on my face?" she asks.

"Me?" I blink. Usually I'm the one with women sitting on my face. I can't even remember the last time someone asked me that. I shake my head.

"Then tell me what you like."

"Honestly? Using your hands is the best way to go, City Girl."

I grin at her using the nickname. She has no idea it comes from my favorite apple variety back on the orchard.

Fuck. I wasn't supposed to think about that tonight. It's bad enough having to say goodbye to someone who was like a mother to me. The responsibility waiting for me back home is enormous, but I know I'm ready. I'll make Benny proud.

"Where'd you just go?" She pulls my face back toward hers.

"Sorry. It's just been a stressful week," I admit.

"Well, then let me help you destress."

Her hand glides down my chest, brushing over my clit before teasing my folds.

"Oh, fuck." I moan as her fingers slip through me gracefully.

I'm wetter than usual—just touching her earlier was enough to wreck me. She's my kryptonite, all soft curves and endless places to explore.

She drags a finger through my folds, circling my clit with her wet hand. My hips buck toward her, but she pushes me back down, her mouth closing over my breast. She swirls her tongue around my nipple, and I moan—louder than usual.

"Come on, Mac. Don't hold back on me."

She looks up at me from between my breasts, hazel eyes glinting.

Before I can say anything, she slides a finger inside me and curls it upward. I curse loudly. She smirks, kissing her way down my stomach.

With one hand, she pumps her finger in and out, the other pressing firmly over my pubic bone. The pressure is dizzying, setting my pussy on fire. My head falls back against the pillows. She pulls out her finger only to add another, pumping both into me, slick with my arousal, as I rock my hips to get more friction.

"Fuck!" I cry out. I'm already so fucking close to coming. I reach to touch her breasts as she moves her thumb across my clit. My breath is heavy, my whimpers turning into moans as she touches me.

"Come on Mac, let me see you come." She looks up at me again, and I force myself to make eye contact with her while I finish.

"Yes! Yes! Yes!" I usually like to scream the woman's name, but that'll do. Holy shit. I'm seeing literal stars as she licks her fingers clean. God, seeing a woman lick *me* off of herself? I'm definitely committing that to memory.

I lie back on the pillows and pull her toward me. "Get on my fucking face. *Now*," I tell her.

"Are you sure?" She looks worried, like she's afraid I can't handle her size or something—which is just crazy because she's shaped like a literal goddess.

"I'm more than sure. Now get up here and let me devour you," I demand.

She smiles, her shyness fading as she settles over my face, and I pull her hips down to my hips. She's still wet. Her clit brushes over my tongue, and her hips buck toward me. Looking up, I see her grabbing and playing with her tits. I try to hold eye contact with her, but it's too much when I feel her juices slipping down my chin. She's so wet—her pussy is sliding effortlessly over my tongue. I moan against her, she tastes too good.

Above me, she's moaning and rocking her hips back and forth to a rhythm. Her hands are pinching her nipples, and her eyes are shut as she enjoys the moment. Maybe she can come easier than she thinks. She probably just needs to relax a little bit. I think she's teetering on the edge of release, but then her eyes shoot open, and she grabs her leg.

"Crap! Leg cramp!" She falls to the side of me, off my face, and stretches out her knee.

"Are you okay?" I can feel how wet my mouth is from her, but there's nothing to discreetly wipe it with.

"Yes, just a leg cramp. Probably from sitting so much on the train." She winces. I'm sure wearing those heels all day don't help either, but now isn't the time to mention them.

"Do you need ice?"

"No, I'll probably be fine. But I think the mood has shifted." She frowns.

"Totally understand. Do you want me to stay?"

"No!" she yells way too quickly. I laugh it off, but damn that kind of stung. "Sorry, my family is coming here in the morning. I don't need them seeing my one-night stand leaving."

"Of course." I nod. That makes me feel a little better. And it isn't like I could stay all night anyway. I have to get up in the morning to arrange the funeral home flowers. Fuck. Well, there goes all the work I put into not thinking about it.

"I'll...thanks for tonight." I struggle with what to say after I've dressed.

"Bye, Mac." She giggles and I let myself out, heading toward the bar.

THREE

Bells

I really hate funerals. I mean, I know nobody likes them, but I especially hate them. It's just a bunch of strangers gathering to say things they never said when the person was alive. I haven't been to one since I was a kid and lost the last of my grandparents—until today. Now, my mother's sister has died, and we've all been swept upstate for a funeral where I don't know a soul.

My family is huge—cousins, aunts, and uncles I only see once a decade, at family reunions or funerals. I'm barely close with my own parents, let alone everyone else. But apparently it "wouldn't look good" if I wasn't here. My parents insist on keeping up appearances. They're even pretending that they are still married, even though they've been living in separate houses for the last five years.

I remember meeting my aunt once or twice as a kid, but I couldn't tell you much about her. My mother never talks about her family, and truthfully, I never asked. I've always been fine on my own. Which is why putting on a forced smile and hugging people who are basically strangers is not how I want to spend my day. Of course I feel bad she died, but I barely knew her—I can't even fake tears.

I know why my mother really wanted to come—especially with my father on her arm. My aunt had money. She had some farm business upstate that apparently did well, and my mother wants her hands on the inheritance money. It's sad, and frustrating, to say the least.

When the funeral procession ends, my parents start making small talk with family members. I slip outside to check my phone. Too many work emails have piled up in the last few hours to ignore. As I'm about to reply, my mother brushes my shoulder with her manicured hand.

"It's time for the will reading, dear," she says softly. Her hand gently squeezes my shoulder, but there's no emotion behind her actions.

"I'll hang out here until you're ready," I say.

"The lawyers requested your presence. It's possible she left you something too."

"Oh." My stomach twists. What could she have possibly left me?

I follow my parents into a back room in the funeral home, where a lawyer, a few extended relatives, my parents, and I gather around a large rectangular table like we're in a business meeting.

The lawyer quickly names everyone listed in the will and is about to begin when someone barges in.

"I have a right to be in there!" The blonde woman jerks her arm out of the guard's grasp.

"Matilda, we talked about this," the lawyer says calmly.

My stomach drops. It's the woman from last night—Mac. The woman who almost made me come. What the hell is she doing here? Did she know my aunt?

"I have a right to know who got it if it wasn't me," she snaps.

"Fine, but you must stay quiet." The lawyer motions to a chair.

She sits in the back, gripping the arms of the chair so tightly I can see her knuckles whiten. I risk one glance her way, but she doesn't seem to notice me.

"Firstly," the lawyer reads, "Miss Blake asked that a donation be made in her name to the following local charities: Sapphire Falls Animal Shelter, Sapphire Falls Housing Authority, and the Sapphire Falls LGBTQ+ Youth Home. The amounts are to be determined by the family. Secondly, she requested that the remains of her trust fund, inheritance, and savings be split evenly among her living relatives."

I keep sneaking glances at the blonde in the back. She doesn't look upset—so what is she waiting for? It was stupid that we agreed not to exchange names last night. If we had, I'd know who she was with one quick Google search. Then again, maybe last night wouldn't have happened.

A flash of heat coils low in my belly, and I'm too embarrassed to admit—even to myself—that I'm turned on just thinking about her.

"And lastly," the lawyer continues, "I leave Sapphire Falls Apple Orchard to my niece, Arabella Kennedy. I hope she will take care of it in the ways I always thought she would."

My jaw drops. My family all turns to stare at me. My aunt left me an orchard?

"Uh—" I'm about to speak when Mac—Matilda, whatever her name is—storms out. I guess that's what she was waiting to hear. At least I know she's not a long-lost relative. Aunt Blake didn't have kids.

"We will need you to sign the following forms," the lawyer says, sliding a stack of papers toward me. My name sits at the top, clear as day. "Once you do, the orchard will be in your name."

"I don't know the first thing about running an apple orchard."

"Miss Blake was quite confident you'd figure it out. There are more details in this folder about what it entails, but you can decline the property if you're not interested."

"I guess… yeah." My voice is faint.

"In the case of your declining, the orchard will be donated to the town and sold to the highest bidder."

"What?!" my family cries in unison.

My head spins. I came here to support my mother and keep up appearances. I didn't expect to inherit anything—let alone a whole orchard. Now I'm wondering if there's more than just apples? Were there animals too?

"I'll take responsibility for it—for now. I don't want it going to the highest bidder."

"Very well. I'll just need to see your ID, and we can start the paperwork."

I hand over my wallet. As the lawyer takes copies and the rest of my family signs their papers, I wonder what the hell I'm going to do with an orchard. My mother will kill me if I turn it down, but maybe she'll buy me out. Then I can finally buy that summer house in the Hamptons.

When we finish, my mother agrees to meet me outside. Before I leave, the lawyer stops me. He's older, with dark gray hair and a thin mustache—like a slim Santa Claus who shaved for the summer.

"There's one more thing," he says. "In taking this over, you're also agreeing not to turn the orchard over to anyone else in the family. Miss Blake was very clear: if you don't want it, it's not to stay in the family."

"What? Why?"

"To put it politely, Miss Blake said she grew this place from nothing and didn't want it in the hands of those only looking to make a profit. She created something special here, Miss Kennedy, and she wants it cared for."

"Okay," I say, nodding slowly.

"Here's the key to the main house and all the information you might need. You'll also meet the main farmhand, Matilda. She lives on the property along with several others. It's up to you if they stay, but they must be given thirty days' notice if you want them out."

"Okay. And if I do decide to sell?"

"You'd need to contact me and a local realtor. I can give you some numbers."

"Sure."

"I know this is a lot to process," he says. "Take the weekend, then visit the orchard. Things will look different when you see it in person."

"Okay."

I nod, but my mind is made up. It's not like I'm keeping it. I live in New York City. I have a job, a life. I'm up for a promotion. There's no way I'm uprooting myself to run an orchard.

But why me? Why did she pick me? She knew how greedy my family was. How did she know I wouldn't be just like them?

I take a deep breath and brace myself to face my parents. I know they'll have a million questions. All I want is a stiff drink.

As I step outside, my parents nearly pounce.

"You're not really thinking of running that orchard, are you?" my mother snaps. Her tone makes it sound like an accusation.

"I'm… not sure," I admit. "It either stays with me, or it's sold. It's complicated."

"She kept my name off the deed, didn't she?" my mother asks, her face falling when I don't answer right away.

"She did. She wanted it kept in the family, but she thought I'd be the one to honor that."

"Are you kidding me?! I've been telling her for years—we could've made a real profit. Why wouldn't she want me to handle it?"

"I don't know." I nod anyway. It's easier than arguing.

"You do know she has a bunch of people living on the property, right?"

"Yes. I told the lawyer I'd go up there and get a better sense of everything first."

"And what, you'll just forget about your family?"

"Aunt Blake was my family," I shoot back. "And people

relied on her. I'm not throwing them out. I don't want them homeless and jobless."

My mother exhales sharply. "Well, I can't argue with that," she says finally, turning toward my father.

The rest of my relatives, who were standing close enough to overhear, file out as well. I watch them go, shaking my head. They already got their money. It's never enough for them. If they can't have everything, they're not happy. Meanwhile, everything they have has been handed to them on a silver platter.

FOUR

Tilly

"**Y**ou've got to be fucking kidding me." I storm out of the office and head home in my truck. I cannot fathom facing anyone else right now.

How the hell could she do that to me? Benny had been like a second mother to me. Truthfully, a *better* mother than the one I had. Kicking me out at seventeen after finding me with a girl in my bed was enough to send me running for the hills. Benny had taken me in, and I'd worked for her ever since. I always thought the farm would eventually be mine, and I'd run it. She'd always alluded to that, so when she got sick, I never thought twice about taking care of her. She didn't tell her family, and they weren't interested in much besides a piece of her inheritance.

Why the fuck would she leave it to her? You've got to be kidding me. In all the years I've worked there, I hadn't seen this woman once. So it wasn't like they were close or anything. If anything, the woman seemed just as surprised. Had I known her last name last night, I never would've hooked up with her. I thought she was just a random ass tourist stopping on her way back down from the city. Why did I go along with her idea to not exchange names?

I storm into the house the second I'm back on the property. I can't even say *my* house anymore, because everything is up in the air. We'll probably only have thirty days or less to vacate the premises. Sighing, I start piling things into a random box. I'm not sure where I'll go, but it's clear…I need to leave. I need to go somewhere else. I really don't want to be here when the new owners arrive. Most of my friends are on the property, too, so it isn't like I can ask to stay with them.

"Tills? Are you here?" My best friend, Hattie comes up the stairs.

"I'm here," I call back from my bedroom.

"What's going on?" She looks around the messy room in confusion.

"Why aren't you at the funeral?" I ask, ignoring her question.

"Well, it was mostly over, and Ollie was a bit overwhelmed by all the people. He's in the backyard running around with the chickens." Hattie smiles.

I glance out the window and see her six-year-old running around with the chickens. He's making chicken sounds and holding his arms up like wings. It's arguably adorable.

"Benny left the house to some distant relative." I sigh, plopping on the bed.

"What?! I thought it was going to you." Hattie's eyebrows furrow.

"Yeah, that's what I thought too. I'm too angry to understand this." I lie back on the bed.

"That doesn't make any sense. Do you think it's some sort of mistake?"

"I did, but her lawyer says the paperwork is exactly what she asked for," I grumble.

"So, what happens now? I can't move Ollie. He loves being homeschooled here. And you know what happens when he can't run around—imagine having to be in school almost eight hours a day," Hattie whispers.

"I know. I just know it's being taken over. But they could decide to sell or keep it or hire someone else to sell it." I sigh.

"I wish we knew more," Hattie says quietly. "I barely saw you last night, though. Did you have fun?"

"No." I grit my teeth. "The woman I hooked up with last night happens to be the woman who just inherited the orchard."

"WHAT?!" Hattie spins around from looking out the window to face me again. "How? What? That's insane. Once again, how?"

"We didn't exchange names last night. I thought she was some random woman. I didn't do a formal background check, but now I wish I did."

"Well, did you do a good job? Like would she consider letting us live here because of your skills? You're always bragging, so they have to be good for something," Hattie teases.

"Now is not the time for jokes!" I groan.

"I mean, did she know who you were? Or that she was getting this place?"

"I don't think so. She looked pretty shocked at the lawyer's meeting. But I don't really know her well enough to say," I say, thinking back to earlier.

"Okay, well then maybe she's reasonable, and you can convince her with your charm to not give up on this place."

"You think I have enough charm to convince her not to go back to her cushy job in the city and instead take up being a farmhand on an apple orchard?" I raise an eyebrow.

"I thought you didn't know that much about her?" Hattie raises an eyebrow back.

"She said she's from the city, and she's dressed like someone out of *The Devil Wears Prada*. It's not hard to guess she has a nice job." I wave her off.

"I see." Hattie nods.

Benny let Hattie move into the neighboring house on the property seven years ago when she was pregnant with Ollie. Her very religious parents kicked her out for getting pregnant out of wedlock. Benny gave her a job as the orchard's official veterinarian. Hattie was only a few credits shy of the title, and Benny convinced her to keep going to get her certificate, with the promise of free room and board.

Hattie has always been easygoing—and she calls me out on my shit. I don't know why I enjoy being called out like that, but I do. She's a better mom to Ollie than either of us had while growing up, and he brings more joy to this place than she does. I never imagined enjoying having a kid around all the time, but now I'm proudly Aunt Tilly, and I can't imagine my life without him. Which is why the thought of moving hurts so much worse than just having to find a new place. I'll probably have to move away from them too.

"There has to be some kind of law against this sort of thing. Like we have to have some sort of rights, right?" Hattie asks, pulling me from my thoughts.

"You'd think so, but I have no idea." I sigh.

"I have to go put Ollie to bed, but as soon as he's down I'll come over with some food and my brainstorming glasses," Hattie says before leaving.

"Ugggggh," I groan, closing my eyes.

I wish I could talk to Benny and get some sort of explanation about what's going on here. The one person I want to talk to about this just isn't around anymore. The grief I feel is weird. I was with her until the very end, so of course I miss her, but I'm also so angry. How the hell could she leave this place in the hands of someone who will probably sell it for a nickel? I don't have any hope about the woman saving the place. Hattie tends to be more hopeful than I am. I'm realistic, because most of the time, if you give people the benefit of the doubt, you're the one who gets hurt.

My phone alarm goes off, and I realize it's feeding time for the horses. I don't have it in me to feed them tonight, but it's not like I'll let them go hungry just to prove a point. I get off the bed and change into my work clothes—boots and all. Heading outside, I toss on a baseball cap to keep my hair out of my eyes. It's late spring, so although they're welcome out of the barn, the horses often stay inside all day. We haven't had too many people stop by for visits, so I get it.

I ring the bell, letting them know it's time for dinner, and grab the water pail first. Getting fresh water from the sink, I make sure everyone has a good supply for the night. It's rare they ever finish it all, but I don't want them getting hot at night. We have six horses, all varying ages, who take the same amount of food. One by one, I make sure everyone's in their assigned stall and lock them in for the night. I don't want them getting into any mischief while I'm sleeping. Then I get each one food and pet their manes to tell them goodnight. I don't bother locking up the barn—no one ever comes on the property, and it's not like someone's going to steal our horses.

The lights at Hattie's house flicker off as she puts Ollie to bed, the only remaining light being the one in his bedroom. It's a night-light, but it's bright enough to see from the barn. He's still getting over being afraid of the dark, so for now he sleeps with the light on. Heading back into the house, I get changed and wait in the living room for Hattie. The front door's unlocked, and because the houses are close enough together, she can bring the baby monitor over for Ollie in case he needs something.

I put on some water for mac and cheese. I'm suddenly starving from the hard labor. Just as I'm draining the pasta, I hear someone knock at the front door.

Confused, I call out, "It's open!" Hattie doesn't usually knock.

But the knock continues. I can't hear if she says anything, but maybe she needs help carrying something in? I put the pasta back in the pot and head for the front door. When I open it, I'm shocked to find my one-night stand on my porch. My stomach turns sour as I see her smiling at me. Doesn't she know how much grief she's causing us?

"Hey, I didn't realize you lived here," she says.

"Yeah, well. I do." I cross my arms and lean against the front doorframe.

"I was just hoping to chat with whoever's in charge. I was told a few people live on the property, and they told me to come here." She's still dressed in her black dress from the funeral. She didn't even stop home to change first?

"You couldn't even wait a night?" I scoff.

"I'm supposed to be back home tomorrow. So it would be easier…" Her mouth forms a line, and she waits for me to say something. But I don't, because I'm still pretty pissed. Mostly at myself for sleeping with her. I feel like I let my guard down accidentally.

"I guess I'll just come back then." She sighs and turns to walk down the front steps.

"I can show you around. I don't want you getting lost or anything," I grumble.

"Thank you."

"Just give me a minute." I sigh and head inside to grab my phone. I make sure all the flames on the stove are off and then put my boots on before meeting her outside.

"I'm Bells, by the way. I don't think we've been properly introduced." She smiles and offers me a hand. I just stare at it until she drops it awkwardly.

"Tilly." I don't offer anything else.

"I can see you're upset about this. I honestly didn't know my aunt was going to do this. She never said anything to me. We haven't even spoken in a few years," Bells says.

I scoff. She's just making this worse. Way to push the knife in even deeper—Benny didn't even know this woman. She isn't some relative she was secretly close with. She's a stranger—one who just happened to share the same bloodline. I'm pissed. I'll get us through this tour as soon as possible, and hopefully she'll be back on her way to the city. I can't stand thinking about her actually selling this place.

FIVE

Bells

I get the feeling things aren't going to be easy working with Tilly. She already hates me, and I can't say I blame her. This is unexpected for me too, but the way she's looking at me is terrifying. I'm glad I texted my best friend, El, before I got here. It feels like the beginning of a serial-killer movie. Not that I really think she'll kill me. But she's basically an angry stranger.

I follow behind her along the dirt path, glad I opted for my gym sneakers. I had a feeling heels wouldn't do me any good here; turns out, I was right.

"That's the barn. We have six horses, but I already said goodnight, so we're not going in there. That way is their pen where they run around during the day," Tilly says.

"Do horses have a bedtime?" I joke, but Tilly just stares at me.

"Along this road, we have Hattie's house. She's the on-call vet for the animals. She's a single mom who lives there with her son. And there's another house where Lina lives—she owns the bakery you see to the right."

I can't tell if she's laying it on thick or just trying to give as much detail as possible.

"The farther we go down this path leads you to the actual orchards. We have six varieties of apples that grow yearly. It's usually my job to tend to them. That's not something that can be taught overnight or explained in a tour."

"Got it." I nod. Clearly, this isn't going to be a smooth transition.

"And you stay in that house?" I motion to the red one closest to the barn.

"Yes."

"Where did my aunt stay?"

"The first house on the property—the white one? That was hers," Tilly says, her jaw tight.

"Got it." I nod again.

I look toward the apple fields and feel nostalgic for my summers here as a kid. I don't remember much—except eating so many apples that my stomach hurt. My aunt and I made apple pie and helped the people who worked here. My cousins often stayed with us, now that I think about it. I guess our parents would drop us off for the summer. It's beautiful. The entire place looks like something out of a Hallmark movie.

But it's not like I'm going to uproot my life for this place.

Not that I necessarily have much to go back home to. Today I found out that my ex, Taylor, got the promotion I wanted. Now she's going to be in charge of me at work—which is the last thing I want. So it's not like I'm looking forward to going home tomorrow.

"We do have rights as far as kicking us out. None of us have written leases, but I'm sure we could find the paperwork Benny had for us. We're not leaving without a fight," Tilly says, breaking the silence.

"I'm not looking to evict anyone. I don't know what my plan is for this place, but I definitely wouldn't leave anyone without a place to work or live. I wanted to see it for myself, meet the people who work here, and do some research," I explain.

"Oh." Tilly's shoulders relax.

"I know we don't know each other, but since I'm the new owner, that's going to have to change."

"Great," Tilly says sarcastically.

A brunette waves at us, and Tilly waves back.

"Who's that?" I ask.

"That's Hattie, the vet," Tilly says.

That doesn't answer my real question, but I guess it's none of my business.

"Can I meet her?" I ask.

"Sure."

We walk back toward the houses. Hattie is sitting on her front porch and reading a book. A glass of wine rests on the table next to her, along with a baby monitor. I guess her son must still be young if she's using that. When she sees us walking up, she puts her book down and meets us at the bottom of her steps.

"Hey, how's it going?" She eyes me suspiciously. Her short, cropped black curls frame her face, freckles scattered across her cheeks and down her thighs. I recognize her from the funeral.

"Hi, I'm Bells—the new owner." I reach out to shake her hand, and her smile fades.

"I'm Hattie." She shakes my hand but looks anxiously between Tilly and me.

"She asked to see the place, so I was giving her a quick tour," Tilly says.

"I just wanted to see the place myself," I add.

"My son's sleeping, or I'd accompany y'all. It's really a beautiful place, especially when the apples are in season and the leaves are changing," Hattie says with a smile.

"I recall." I smile.

"Well, we should get going. Your tour is finished, and you should get to packing before you head home tomorrow," Tilly says, clearly trying to rush me out.

"Why don't you stop by tomorrow morning? Lina makes the best apple turnovers, and we all usually have breakfast together. Then you can meet a few of the day staff, too," Hattie suggests.

I ignore how Tilly shoots daggers at her friend for inviting me.

"I'd love that. I want to see all this place has to offer."

"Perfect. We stop for breakfast around eight a.m. Sound good?" Hattie asks.

"Yes." I nod.

"Great," Tilly says through gritted teeth.

It's honestly a little funny at this point. I know she doesn't like me, but it's not like I'll get the orchard and disappear. I have to make real decisions now—whether I want to sell or what I'm going to do with the place. I can't leave it in the hands of complete strangers and hope for the best.

Getting to know all the staff and what this place looks like in the daylight is a great idea. I also need to stop by my aunt's house and see where she keeps the financial books. I have a key to a file cabinet from the lawyer, but I don't know where it is exactly.

"I'll see you both tomorrow then. Thanks for the tour." I say goodbye and head for the cab I paid to wait for me. It's costly but more efficient than calling it back. I knew I wouldn't be here long.

When I get in the cab, I start a few Google searches. I'm curious what this place originally sold for and what it might go for now. I can't find specifics, but getting a rundown of the website, the social media accounts, and the typical business methods they use can't hurt.

Unfortunately, all I find are Google hours—no Instagram account, not even a cheap website. This place is in need of my help and a complete makeover. How can we get new customers here if no one even knows it exists? There's no way they're relying solely on locals to get them through the year.

By the time I get back to my family's apartment, I have a better idea of what the orchard looks like. To my surprise, when I open the front door, my parents and some of my aunts and uncles are inside. Thank God I managed to hide my dirty clothes and make the bed before I left. The apartment isn't big, but it holds my two aunts, three uncles, and my parents.

"Finally! We were waiting for you," my mother says, hanging up the phone.

"What's going on?" I tread carefully. I have a good idea this is about the orchard, but I don't know what exactly. I take off my sneakers and place them by the door, even though everyone else hasn't bothered to.

"We talked to the family lawyer, and we think there may be a way to get around Benny's will," my mother says cheerfully.

"What?" I try not to react too strongly. I don't want them to think I'm hurting the family. That's how Benny became the family's black sheep.

"Your mother found out that if you sign the deed over to your father instead of your mother, we'll be able to access the land and sell it for three times its worth," my aunt Sophie adds.

Of course this is about the money.

"I see." I pause, trying to decide where to go from here.

"Why are you dirty? Did you fall?" my mother asks, looking me over.

Usually, when I'm around them, I make sure there isn't a hair out of place. It's something my mother instilled in me from a young age—you can never make a second first impression, so you must always look your best. I glance down and see dirt on my shin and the bottom of my skirt. I must've picked it up getting into the cab.

"I was actually just at the orchard. I was curious about the land." It's not a complete lie.

"Perfect. What did you think? It shouldn't take long to get everyone off the property. I think only five or six actually live on the land," my mother says with a smile.

"I thought we weren't going to evict anyone?" I frown.

"Well, it might be easier to sell if we didn't have anyone living on it," my uncle adds.

"I see," I repeat. I don't know how to get what I want without losing my parents' respect in this moment.

"Would you like us to send you the lawyer's number so you

can set up a meeting? I know you're headed back to the city tomorrow, but really, the quicker we resolve this, the better. Don't you think?" my mother asks.

I look around the room at all the eyes on me and sigh. I can't let them down, but I'm not ready to give up on this either. Aunt Blake left this for me for a reason—something I don't fully understand yet. But seeing it tonight only cements what I already know: I can't let it fall into my family's greedy hands.

"I actually was thinking about looking into the finances, doing some renovations before we sell," I say quickly. I'm talking out of my ass, but she doesn't need to know that. "I think there's quite a bit we could do beforehand and make more than what you said. And we'd want to get the most for this place, right?"

I'm laying it on thick, but that's what works for my family.

"Hmm, that does make sense. It's pretty run-down, from what I imagine. But we don't want you spending too much to fix it up," my mom says.

"Of course. I'll budget everything. I just think it could be spruced up before we go for the hard sell," I say.

I know I'm only buying myself some time, but it's better than nothing right now.

"You're right." My mom smiles.

"It's smart. Definitely better to sell as an established company than a fixer-upper," my uncle adds.

I just nod as they start talking about timelines and specifics and everything else. All I know is that I will not be staying here after tonight. There's no way I'm coming home and being ambushed by my family again. I'll find somewhere else to stay, even if it's just temporary.

I have to figure out a way to get the place back to its former glory.

SIX

Tilly

"Why the hell would you invite her back tomorrow?" I glare at Hattie after Bells is gone.

"Because she seems reasonable and maybe if we show her the place and all it has to offer, she won't make us homeless." Hattie frowns.

"Or she could see it's not doing as well as it should be and kick us out even faster." I groan.

"You don't know that."

"You don't know she's reasonable, you met her for two minutes." I sigh.

"So you know her better because you had your tongue inside her?" She raises an eyebrow, and I blush.

"I'm just saying. I've seen plenty of business types come through here that look harmless and then try to screw us over in the long run."

"But not everyone is like that, Tills. You have to give people the benefit of the doubt sometimes." She sighs.

"Fine. But I'm not being nice to her. I'm keeping my guard up because I'm telling you—I do not have a good feeling about this."

"That's okay, you aren't much of a Suzy sunshine anyway." She laughs.

"Are you coming over soon?" I ask, changing the subject.

"Yes, let me get the bottle of wine, and I'll be right over. Did you eat?" She has a tendency to mother me, even if she doesn't mean to.

"I was making mac and cheese, but it's probably shit by now," I grumble.

"I'll bring over some leftovers. I made meatloaf tonight."

"Thank you."

I head back to my place, kicking my boots aside and heading for the kitchen. I dump the overcooked and cold noodles into the garbage and grab a beer from the fridge. Tossing the cap in the trash, I take a large chug. My hand grips the edge of the counter, and I clench my jaw. Why does she have to be so freaking nice? I had hoped she'd be as bitchy as I made her out to be in my head. Then I wouldn't have to worry about liking her when she was the one person standing in the way of what I want. Of course she's gorgeous. It isn't going to be easy to hold my stance.

"Damn, you look more angry than you did before," Hattie says as she walks into my kitchen.

She places the wrapped plate on the counter and offers me her arms. I want to say yes, but I know that I shouldn't, so I shake my head and take another sip of the beer. Hattie told me, not too long ago, that she has feelings for me, and although I don't feel the same, I've been trying not to make it weird. The truth is, I just don't see her that way, and I'm definitely not in any place to want to be a parent to a child. I had let her down gently, and things mostly went back to normal—except times like this, when I'm not sure if I should let her just hug me or not. I just don't want to give her any false hope when there's nothing here.

"Maybe I'm not up to company tonight," I mumble between sips.

"That's fine, but you at least need to eat. And promise you'll meet us in the morning," she insists.

"Fine." I roll my eyes.

Hattie squeezes my arm gently before leaving, and I sigh. I don't want to kick her out, but I can't handle anyone else's feelings right now. Finishing the beer, I pull off the plastic wrap on the plate and put it in the microwave. Two minutes later, I'm sitting on the couch, fresh beer on the table, and a hot plate of food in my hands. I toss on an old re-run of *Friends*—just something to take my mind off things.

I know I'm angry, but I haven't been *this* angry in a long time. Not since…nope, not going there. I did my time working through that and going over it again won't do me any good. Maybe this is just my way of grieving Benny. I'm angry and upset about her dying, and now I'm losing my last piece of her. I don't care what Bells said, it's clear she will have to make some changes to this place. I'm definitely not as optimistic as Hattie.

If it wouldn't give her the wrong idea, I'd just tell Hattie to pack up her and Ollie's things so we could find a place together. But everything is complicated now, and I don't want to further complicate everything by suggesting we leave together. She's my best friend, but I'm attempting to maintain boundaries.

Angrily, I turn off the TV and decide to head to bed. I'm two beers in, and I should probably get some sleep instead of stewing in my feelings. Plus, I have to get up early tomorrow to meet everyone for coffee. I like our little group getting together, but this is not exactly what I had in mind. I don't want to drink coffee and eat muffins with my enemy.

In the morning, I grab a shower and get dressed, hoping to get this meet and greet over with. But as soon as I walk into Lina's bakery, it's clear that's not going to happen. Bells is here, smiling and chatting with Lina and Hattie as if they're old friends. They all laugh about something, and I feel like I'm left out of a secret joke. Ollie is sitting at the table coloring and eating the end of a chocolate chip muffin, so he doesn't notice me. The morning crew for the orchard is here, just like every Monday, when we have a weekly meeting before starting our day. Usually, Benny says any updates and then tells everyone to get to work after they eat. I guess it's my job to step up and take over today. I feel a bit of pride swelling in my chest.

"Good morning, everyone," I say loudly. Everyone turns toward me and rushes to find a seat.

Bells stands in the back of the room with Lina and Hattie, who whisper something quietly to her.

"I know this is a bit of a change, and I know we're all still grieving. Benny wasn't just our boss; she was like family to us. So if anyone needs any extra time off or needs someone to talk to, please find me after. We're open to the public today, so if you can work, please do. I'll be—"

Bells makes her way to the front of the room, smiling. "Excuse me."

I try not to glare at her in front of everyone, but she's literally interrupting me mid-sentence.

"Yes?"

"I just wanted to introduce myself. I'm Bells Kennedy. My aunt Benny left me this orchard, so as the new owner I'll be around a bit today and then popping up in the future. I'm really trying to get a feel for the vibe of this place, so don't mind me. But if you have any questions, don't hesitate to ask." She purses her bright red lips that match the red top she's wearing. It's buttoned all the way except for one at the top, leaving enough cleavage to tease me. I remember all too well what she looks like undressed.

"Thanks," I say plainly. "Now, back to—"

Bells interrupts me again. "And for the record, I will not be getting rid of any jobs or asking anyone to move. I'm simply trying to evaluate the property as a whole and how it works."

I stare at her until she nods at me, like I'm allowed to speak again. The nerve of this woman. "Lina asks that you keep the kids away from the greenhouse out back. It is locked, but we'd like to keep the general public away from it as well."

Lina is legally growing weed to make a variety of edibles for her bakery, something Benny was quite excited to start the process of. We're taking every precaution when it comes to visitors on the orchard, especially kids. But it doesn't hurt to have the reminder. Bells gives me a weird look, but I go on. It's mainly a few old memos, and then I dismiss everyone to finish breakfast. No one comes to talk to me, so I guess they're all grieving on their own time.

"Your friends are so nice," Bells says to me when I don't say anything.

"They are." I nod. She opens her mouth to speak, but I walk toward the bakery counter before she can. I'm not in the mood to make small talk with her right now. Maybe after a cup of coffee it won't be so bad.

"Your usual?" Lina asks from behind the counter.

"Yes. With an extra espresso shot, please." Lina raises an eyebrow but doesn't say anything while she makes the drink. Breakfast is something that the orchard covers for everyone, so I don't have to pay, but I do put a five-dollar bill in the decorated tip jar.

"You okay?" Lina asks as she passes me the cup of iced coffee.

"Just a bit on edge," I say quietly.

"She's nervous about all the changes," Hattie adds.

"I'm fine. I just don't believe everything is going to be fine like she's saying. Her family is notorious for wanting money. I don't trust her."

It didn't click who she is until she said her last name is

Kennedy. They own a chain of hotels across the states as well as a large part of the buildings in town. Benny changed her last name to Blake at some point before I moved here. I know she was connected to the Kennedys, but she didn't like to broadcast that. The only times she spoke of them was to condemn their business practices and complain about how all they cared about was money. Which makes absolutely no sense why she left the orchard to one of them. Wasn't that exactly the opposite of what she wanted?

"Just because she's related to them doesn't mean they have the same values," Hattie points out.

"I'll believe that when I see it." I scoff. I take a sip of my coffee just as Ollie runs over.

"Mama, can I have some water?" He looks up at Hattie with a face full of chocolate.

"Of course, but let's wipe that face of yours." Hattie grabs a wipe from her purse and cleans him off in seconds.

"Who's this little one?" Bells joins the group before I can escape.

"This is my son, Ollie. Ollie, say hi to Bells," Hattie smiles.

"Hi." He has a tendency to be shy at first.

"Very nice to meet you, Ollie, and what do you do on the orchard?" Bells kneels to talk to him.

"I help my mama," he says, smiling proudly.

"That's the best kind of help," Bells winks at him. I can feel myself starting to smile, and I stop it. I'm not going to fall for her tricks and be blindsided at the last second. I won't let that happen.

"Tilly, would you be able to help me? I was hoping you might know how to get into Benny's house." Bells stands and turns to me.

"What? Why?"

"It's where I'll be staying for the time being, but I don't seem to have a key in the stuff the lawyer gave me. I thought you might have a spare key, so I don't need to find a locksmith," she explains.

"I thought you lived in the city," I say curtly. What the hell is she doing staying at Benny's house?

"I do, but the orchard just became my priority. I'll be working remotely until I decide to head back," she says. "So, do you have a key?"

My head starts to spin as I realize Benny is gone and this woman is taking over even faster than I thought she would.

SEVEN

Bells

"This was my key, but I guess I don't really need one anymore," Tilly says, handing me a lanyard with a pride flag and a key on the end.

"Thanks." I smile.

She still hasn't given me an ounce of a smile or even a look my way since the funeral. But I'll eventually win her over. Once I decided to stay in Aunt Blake's house, I knew winning Tilly over would be part of the long game. My parents and family think I headed back to the city; meanwhile, I'll be here for the time being. I can do the renovations and fix what needs to be fixed while also keeping my job in the city. I'm not lying about working remotely, but now I can get two things done at once. I put out feelers to sublet my place, and I'll head down at some point this week to grab more clothes. But I have a feeling the things in my closet won't help me fit in here anyway.

"I'm sure the fridge is rancid because we sort of forgot to clean it after…"

"No worries, I'll make sure I get to that today then," I reassure her.

"It's a pretty big house for one person," Tilly muses.

"Didn't Benny live here alone?"

Tilly makes a face and then nods. I guess we're back to nonverbal communication. I thought we were finally making some progress.

"I guess if you need anything you can ask. I have to get started on the morning feedings and rounds on the orchard," Tilly says.

"Thanks, I appreciate your help." I smile.

Tilly nods and heads out the front door, closing it behind her. I knew my aunt was sick, but I don't have much more to go on besides that. I didn't bother asking my mother what illness she had because there's a good chance she doesn't know. So seeing the medical equipment set up in the living room is a little surprising. I guess she was insistent on spending her last days here. I can't blame her—it's not like I'd want to be sent to some home if I could avoid it.

I tie up my hair and look for some garbage bags. I manage to find some black ones and start getting rid of all the things I know I won't need. It's not like the place is dirty, but there are some opened supplies or things we can't donate.

I'm more sentimental than my family, so I know they aren't holding out for any family photos or anything. But at some point, they may ask about her house, and I'd like to clear it out before they do. I can at least salvage all the important things they'd probably overlook. I find some empty boxes in the closet and pack up all the unused medical equipment. I make a check-list in my phone of things I need to do, including calling the local hospital to see if they can pick this stuff up.

My aunt's taste in furniture and decorations surprisingly isn't bad. I was expecting mix-and-match old-lady thrifted stuff, but in reality, it's all very cozy and fall-themed. Her favorite color must have been orange because it's a common theme here.

My phone rings as I'm finishing packing up one half of the living room.

"Hello?"

"Why do you sound out of breath? Were you having sex?" my best friend El asks from the other end.

"What? No. I was lifting heavy boxes." I laugh.

"Oh, well, I was bored at work, and I missed you."

"Shouldn't you be working on a case?" She's an incredibly sought-after lawyer in the city, so it's not like she has a boring career.

"Are you my boss? No, but seriously, when are you coming home?"

"I actually… umm… I'll be staying here for the time being." I wince. I didn't want to tell her over the phone, but it all happened so fast.

"What?! That's how I find out my bestie is abandoning me?" She gasps.

"I need to figure out why my aunt left me this place and fix it up. My family wants to suck it dry, but I think it could really be something special," I admit.

El knows all about the orchard and helps me with all the legal questions I have. She reads stuff like this on a daily basis, and some of it makes no fucking sense to me. So it shouldn't be a huge surprise that I want to stay and take over the orchard. Except, I'm the last person on earth to willingly stay in a small town, and I've been itching for a decent coffee all weekend. I haven't gotten around to having one at Lina's because I don't want to insult hers. It's not like all coffee here is bad, but it just isn't as strong as I'm used to.

I'm a city girl through and through. I like being able to walk everywhere, and the fact that I can't leave the property without a car is eventually going to get to me. It's not like I'm suddenly going to learn to drive at my age, but I guess it's something I should consider if I do stay here long term.

"But you're staying there? Like on the farm?" she asks.

"It's not a farm, really…"

"There are animals and trees? Didn't you mention a barn?" she says.

"Yes." I laugh.

"Then it's a farm," she decides.

"Okay, fair. But there's a house—my aunt's house here. It's like three stories, and once I clean it up, it might actually be cute for an Airbnb or something," I say.

"Are you thinking about moving up there?"

"No, I just… there are so many people who relied on my aunt. Without her here, they'd be without everything. She created this little community here, and I don't want to disband that if I don't have to. So I'm hoping I can fix it up a little, make a new website, and then present it to my family as a money maker. Possibly convince them to keep it instead of selling," I explain.

"You know you don't have to convince your family of anything. It's up to you if you want to sell—it actually very specifically says not to sell it to them," she reminds me.

"I know. But it's fine. It's easier this way," I insist.

"Whatever you say." She disagrees with me, but it's one of those things we agree to disagree on. I know better when it comes to my family.

"How's it going with Tara?" I ask, changing the subject.

"Fine." She sighs.

"Is something going on there?" She usually has more to say about her live-in girlfriend.

"It's nothing. I just feel like we're in this rut. I'm sure it's just in my head. I'm sure it'll pass."

I'm not sure if she's trying to convince me or herself. I like Tara and El together, but they never seemed like something long term—just two people who feel content together.

"Shit, I gotta go! My boss is on the floor! Bye! Love you!" She hangs up quickly, and I laugh.

I go back to cleaning up, then crash out on the couch and start online shopping. I need more casual clothing, a pair of boots, sneakers I won't mind getting dirty, and a variety of beauty tools. If I'm staying here, it makes more sense to have it delivered here. I have to check the will to make sure I have the right address.

It's a large order, probably spending more than I should, but when do I ever look at the price tag? My credit card is already loaded into the app before I click on a second app. I need to have some of my stuff packed up and delivered, and I really don't want to do that myself. I know a good moving company that can have my stuff up here within the week, so I schedule that as well.

After cleaning out the kitchen—including the very expired items in the fridge—I place an order for food. I don't know where there's a supermarket, but I don't drive anyway. It won't get here until the end of the week, so hopefully there's takeout nearby that will deliver in the meantime. What restaurants does a small town have anyway? I doubt there's a McDonald's or Wendy's nearby. I'm sure I could convince someone on the orchard to get me groceries earlier if I need, but I don't want to be the new owner who comes in and asks for favors. I know everyone is wary of me, so I'm trying to take it one moment at a time.

Bracing myself, I head upstairs and take count of the bedrooms. On the second floor, I find three and an office that could always be turned into a bedroom. My aunt's bedroom is the one at the end of the hallway, and although I could, I don't feel ready to disturb her things. I find fresh sheets in the closet and make up my bed in the guest room at the other end of the hall.

As I'm putting the pillowcases on, I look out the window on the side wall. Outside, I see a blonde figure on a horse galloping through the fenced-in area by the red barn. I have a feeling it's Tilly. She's in total control. I can't see her face from here, but I have a feeling she's actually smiling.

I wish she and I hadn't gotten off on the wrong foot. She probably doesn't want to talk about our one-night stand, and she definitely doesn't want to talk about my aunt leaving the property to me. I still don't know the extent of their friendship, but I can tell they were close.

I have so many questions I want to ask her, but I can tell she's not ready. Has she lived here long? Was there a romantic aspect between them? I assume not, considering the age difference, but that doesn't mean anything. I didn't even know my aunt was queer until I saw all the pride memorabilia in her room. Of course, now it's too late to ask my aunt, but I hope eventually I can ask Tilly.

She has a wall up, and it's going to take time before she trusts me. I'm sure part of it has to do with grieving my aunt, but the other parts? It's sort of driving me crazy.

She rides the horse around the perimeter and only stops when she reaches the barn again. She hops down, pets the horse, and offers it something yellow. Probably a carrot or apple. I figure she's going to get back to work, but instead she pauses to look around. I see her shoulders rise and fall like she's taking deep breaths.

This must be affecting her more than she's ready to let anyone in on.

It's the people-pleaser in me, wishing I could get people to talk to me. If there's any kind of issue, I always want to fix it. Ever since I was little, I'd play therapist, and people would bare their souls to me. Then I'd do everything I could to make it better. It took me a long time to realize that most of the time, it's none of my business. And that when I try to fix things, I sometimes make them worse.

So instead of walking over to the barn and offering Tilly a chance to talk, I close the curtains and go back to cleaning the house.

EIGHT

Tilly

Bells has only been here a week, and already she's making a mess of everything. It's like she's not only accident-prone but has a tendency to touch and "fix" things that aren't even broken. It's a constant fight with myself not to get involved. I mostly keep to myself, tending to the animals, looking over the orchard as a whole, and fixing any issues people might have.

Although we're open to the public, we get fewer than twenty people a day. And every day, Bells goes around with her little clipboard, noting things down. I can only imagine what it says. I'm sure things aren't up to par for her.

The only good thing is she's traded in her heels for an actual pair of boots and those ridiculous pencil skirts for leggings. The only bad part is how freaking good her ass looks in them—like two ripe apples that catch my eye every time she's around me. It's freaking torture, which is why I'm actively avoiding her at this point. If I see her coming, I excuse myself to literally anywhere else on the orchard.

Hattie and Lina say I'm being childish, but I'm not going to be the one surprised when this nice act ends and she sells the place.

"Hey, Tilly? Can we have a moment to chat?" Bells sneaks up behind me while I'm giving the horses their breakfast.

"Uh, sure." I finish with the last one and slide off my gloves before looking at her.

Her auburn curls are tied up in a tight ponytail, and while she's wearing makeup, it's not as much as the first few times I met her. I can actually see more of her face now. She's wearing those tight-ass leggings and a jacket zipped up to reveal only a hint of cleavage. She has her usual clipboard and a sparkly pen in hand.

"So, there are some things I'd love to go over with you. I've been taking inventory of everything in the last two weeks, and I have some ideas. Of course, I feel you'd know exactly what's possible to actually do—or if it's already been tried." She smiles.

"Okay."

"Do you want to grab a cup of coffee at Lina's and chat about it? It's an extensive list."

"No thanks. I have more to do after this," I lie.

"All right, well, I was thinking of ways to bring in more traffic, and I was thinking about reaching out to my contacts in the city and seeing if they'd have any idea about getting a deal with Metro-North. Maybe a discounted ticket when you buy tickets to the orchard kind of deal."

"You want to bring in city folk?" I scoff. That's not our consumer base at all. We thrive on people from neighboring small towns, not city people who wear heels and makeup and complain about the smells of nature.

"Yes, I think it could be a good way to increase sales and traffic," she says.

"Our consumer base has always been other small-town people. People with kids and pets and such. Why would we shift that to bring in people from the city?" I wrinkle my nose in disgust. I can't help it. I have beef with the city the way New Yorkers have beef with New Jersey.

"First off, I'm from the city, so please don't say it like there's something wrong with that. But second, I know that might be what you usually did, but it couldn't hurt to switch things up," she explains.

"Sure." I leave it at that. I'm not in the mood to argue with her.

"I also thought that it might make sense to have an influencer day. Allow them to come up, experience the place for free, make content, and post it to drive traffic up here as well."

"You want to give away free tickets and an entire day of sales to make money? That doesn't make any sense." I shake my head.

"It would be a way to get people with a strong follower base to do the marketing for free. Why doesn't that make sense?"

She's getting defensive, but I don't care. This is a stupid idea.

"How the hell are New Yorkers and influencers even our base? No one up here has social media, so they wouldn't see all this so-called content anyway." I scoff.

"But the people with families and pets who you claim are your base might have it. And when searching for things to do in the summer and fall, seeing this place as an option would drive traffic to paid days," she explains. Her jaw is clenched, and I can tell she's trying hard not to fight with me.

I have to admit—it's kind of hot to see her teetering on the edge of anger like this.

"You think parents have the time to sit and scroll on social media? Why don't you ask Hattie how often she updates her Instagram? We should be focusing on keeping what we have steady and not worrying about bringing on any new people." I shake my head.

"You really think single parents don't know how to Google? A few posts about this orchard going viral is the difference between a Google search showing this place as the first choice and not being on the list," she says with a bite. "And another thing, the families and consumers you have now aren't cutting it. If you haven't noticed, this is the busiest day we've had all week and there are fewer than thirty people here."

Now I'm the one who's pissed. Is she implying I'm bad at my job? "It's not like this is a mall or some New York pop up—it's a freaking apple orchard. One *your* aunt has run successfully for almost twenty-five years. Are you really going to shit on her legacy weeks after her death?"

Bells looks shocked, mouth agape as she takes in what I've said. "I'm in no way shitting on anyone's legacy. She was *my* family. I'm trying to make sure we survive the next season!"

"Yeah? If you were her family, then where have you been for the last ten years?" I scoff.

Bells doesn't hold back her anger anymore. Lowering her clipboard, she looks at me and says, "Fuck you," before storming off.

I kick the empty bucket next to me, and it topples over with a loud clang. Fuck! Why did I let her get such a rise out of me? I could only imagine my conversation with Hattie later when I tell her about this. I'm going to be fired before she can sell the place, and I'll be begging Hattie to let me sleep on her couch. She just got me so pissed when she walked in here acting like she knew how to run this place better. I knew it was a low blow the moment I said it. I shouldn't have brought up her aunt, but now I'd have to apologize, which is the last thing I feel like doing.

I don't know which way Bells went, so I decide to lay low and hang out in the stables. The horses are able to roam free, their breakfast is there, but they like to lie in the sun and run around after being in all night. They usually graze on their food throughout the day. But I decide to saddle up my horse for a ride. I watched Millie's birth right after moving here. She's a good rider now, and I love taking her out of the pen to the outskirts of the orchard. The other horses are too wild for me to try that, but Millie knows not to try anything. We always stop and get some fresh apples on the way back.

I slide my saddle onto Millie's back, hitch on her harness, and climb up. The only thing I need right now is to relax and not think for a while. Things have been hard since Benny died. I often find myself looking for her or going to knock on her door to tell her something. We communicated all the time without thinking twice about it; it's weird to have to rewire that part of my brain. Because immediately I want to go tell her what a bitch Bells is being and how she shouldn't even be here. But that's the exact reason she's here.

Millie starts riding, and I lead her out the only entrance I can unlock without getting off her. I unhook the lock, and we head toward the open fields. She's fast, but not too fast where I feel sick. If anything, I feel the relaxation I was craving. The wind blows in my hair, the sun is on my face, and I let her take control of direction. There's no one out here, so it's safe for us to run in circles or run whatever way she wants.

The apple trees look so beautiful this way. It's late May now, and they're in full bloom. All the flowers—mostly white and pink—cascade over each tree. It won't be long before the orchard transforms into a fall scene. Every year, it happens quickly. One moment it's spring, and the next I'm wheeling in pumpkins from the patch and smelling Lina baking pumpkin pies.

Each year we had a joint Thanksgiving, all of us and whatever staff didn't have plans gathering at Benny's house. She cooked for hours— a huge turkey, about half a dozen sides, and at least a dozen desserts. The day started before sunrise, and no one went home until after dark. We all took turns with the cooking, cleaning, and sharing.

My stomach lurches thinking about what kind of Thanksgiving we might have this fall. I have a feeling I'll be eating one of those microwavable turkey dinners in whatever shitty apartment I'm living in. Maybe Hattie and I will get together, but no one knows how to cook the way Benny did. Lina can bake, but when it comes to anything savory, she's less than good.

Tears slip down my cheeks without warning. I'm not someone who likes to cry in public, but I've had my fair share of tears behind closed doors. The other day, I bawled when I came across a note Benny had left me. All it said was "Could you bring some milk over?" but seeing her handwriting again made something inside me break.

Grief is like a toddler—a weird thing you can't control, apt to set you off at random times, but also reminding you that what you feel is real. For me, it reminds me how short life can be, and I'm not going to spend any more of it worrying about things I can't change. Benny always looked forward, insisting on not looking back or trying to fix things with her awful family.

I guess it's a good thing I have my savings. I always thought I'd use the money to buy the place from Benny, but now I'll probably have to use it to buy a house or something nearby. Finding a job will be difficult, considering I never went to college and this is the only job I've ever had. Giving any references might be tough.

But I push those thoughts aside. I can't think about that right now. Right now, I need to relax enough to get back to work. Maybe if I show Bells how helpful and needed I am around here, she'll overlook my smart mouth and let me stay.

Here's to hoping, anyway.

NINE

Bells

"How are you coming along?" Lina asks, pouring me a second cup of coffee. I was sitting at one of the back tables working on the budget for this month.

"Good, thanks." I smile.

"If you need anything, just holler." She smiles and touches my back softly. Her long blonde hair cascades down her back in a tight braid. I'm in awe of how long it is and how I never seem to get any of it in my food.

Looking over the budget for this place, I realize it's going to be tough to keep the place running for the next three months— let alone the rest of the season. I don't know what my aunt's plan was or how it got this bad. Was she paying the bills even when she was sick? Did Tilly know how bad things have gotten? She seems to be in charge of most aspects, but maybe my aunt was like the rest of my family and hid her finances. We need to bring in some revenue and fast or there will be no way I can sell this place, let alone keep any of the staff on. I had hoped Tilly would be able to put aside her distaste for me, and we could work together, but it doesn't seem like that's going to happen. She shot down all my ideas without even thinking about them. And then when I called her on it, she insulted me.

Of course it eats at me, knowing my aunt had no family around her when she died. But I also think that might be the way she wanted it. She was never close with my mom or any of their siblings, so it isn't surprising that she didn't reach out. And truthfully, I broke my arm when I was a kid, and my mom was the worst to be around me. She was there for me the first day and then complained any time I talked about being upset with my cast. I was seven and broke my arm on the last day of school; my entire summer was spent in a cast. I actually remember my aunt being someone who understood and figured out one-armed things we could do together that summer.

I'm drinking a hot coffee because when I came in here it was nice and cool. But suddenly I'm hit with a heat wave. I think maybe Lina is cooking something and opened the oven, or someone left the front door open. But as I look around, I notice I'm not the only one looking hot. Several customers get up and leave while the others are using their shirts as fans.

"Hey Lina, what's going on? Why is it so hot in here?" I ask quietly, going up to the counter.

"The AC is out again. Truthfully, we need a new one, but I know it's low on the priority list. Tilly's coming over to fix it— she usually does something that keeps it fine for a few weeks," Lina explains.

I nod. "Okay, maybe let's get everyone else some iced water in the meantime?" I suggest. I don't want anyone passing out on my watch.

"Of course." Lina smiles and heads to the back.

I head back to my table just as Tilly walks in. She's wearing jean overalls, one strap hanging down, and just a black sports bra underneath. Her arm muscles are insanely toned and glisten with sweat. Her blonde hair looks freshly cut, the sides shaved clean and the top messy. If I weren't still so mad at her, I'd want to take her on the counter. But I am, so I avert my eyes and try to focus on the work I'm doing.

Of course, that's pointless because Tilly opens her red toolbox, and I'm like a dog in heat watching her every move. She bends over to look at the air conditioner, and I get a nice view of her toned ass. It must be all the work she does because holy fuck, that ass is not just from squats.

She starts messing around under the air conditioner while Lina stands nearby talking to her. I can't hear their conversation, but I see their lips moving. I refocus on my computer when the screen dims and realize I need to at least look like I'm not staring at my employee.

"Bells! Come here!" Lina waves me over, and I'm terrified I got caught staring.

"What's up?" I try to say casually as I approach them.

I'm standing over Tilly, which makes me think about how good it felt to be sitting on her face that night—which is positively the last thing I should be thinking about. At least it's still hot in here, so I can blame my flushed cheeks on that.

"Tilly and I were just talking about an idea we had." Lina smiles.

"Oh yeah?" I'm happily surprised.

"It's not a big deal." Tilly shakes her head and continues working.

"It was something we thought of but never got around to talking to Benny about. We'd love to throw a masquerade ball on the orchard. Maybe make a themed night of it and throw a party in the gazebo outside?" Lina says happily.

"In the summer?" I'm a little confused—usually that's more of a fall thing.

"No, like maybe in September? Or a Halloween one?" Lina adds.

"I like it. I'll definitely put it on the list."

There's nothing wrong with the idea, but it's not the time or place to let them know we may not even be open by then.

"It was mostly Lina's idea," Tilly says. "So don't bash it on my account."

"I'm not bashing it." I shake my head. "It would just take a lot of planning, and my focus right now is bringing in sales for the summer. But it's definitely not a no," I reassure Lina, glaring at Tilly, who's back to ignoring me.

Lina gives me a soft smile, and I head back to my laptop. I decide once I see the place is back to normal and Tilly is done, I'll head home for the day. I have work for my real job to do, and I don't need to get into it with Tilly about nothing.

I write down the masquerade ball idea in my notes and start packing my stuff up. Tilly finishes, and the air kicks back on, leaving Lina smiling in relief.

I'm placing my mug of cold coffee into the dish bucket when, at the same moment, Tilly stands up and flexes. Her back muscles look magnificent as she reaches for her toolbox, and I miss the bucket, causing the cup to fall and shatter. The loud crash turns every head, and suddenly I'm covered in coffee and ceramic pieces.

"Shit, I'm so sorry," I tell no one in particular as I reach for the biggest shard. I don't realize how sharp it is until it slices through the side of my hand. Blood starts pouring out, and I hold it away from me.

I'm terribly squeamish when it comes to blood—and I've been known to pass out before.

Lina and Tilly rush over, Lina grabbing a broom while Tilly takes my hand. She grabs some napkins and presses them tightly to the cut.

"Fuck, can't you ever be careful?" she mutters under her breath.

"It was an accident." I scoff.

"You're literally the most clumsy person I know. You could take a page out of Bella Swan's book." She chuckles.

"Are you calling me Bella Swan? It was bad enough growing up with a similar name." I groan. Twilight was immensely popular when I was younger, and my name being Arabella didn't stop anyone from calling me Bella.

"I might have to call you that from now on—maybe Lamb for

short." She winks. I hate that I understand the reference exactly. Edward calls Bella a lamb when he says the infamous line, *'so the lion fell in love with the lamb'*.

"Okay, I got the first aid kit, but no one's ever needed this, so I don't actually know what's in it." Lina rushes back.

"Hold her hand away from her so she doesn't see the blood, and I'll look through it," Tilly instructs.

Lina takes over, her grip much looser than Tilly's. Tilly digs through the first aid kit, pulling out alcohol wipes, bandages, and gauze.

Was the cut that deep? Probably just in an annoying spot. I definitely don't want to look and check.

She cleans her hands with the sanitizer on the counter, then opens everything.

"Do me a favor and close your eyes, little lamb. I don't want you passing out too," Tilly teases.

"Fine." I roll my eyes but close them.

Tilly touches my hand, and I feel the air on the cut when she removes the napkins. She wipes it—it stings like hell, but I don't say anything. Then she pats it dry and finally places the bandage on me.

"You can look now," Tilly says.

"Thanks." I wish I didn't have such a blood phobia—it really doesn't help when I'm as clumsy as Tilly says.

"I'll get you some water. You still look pale as a ghost," Lina says.

"Or maybe a vampire," Tilly teases quietly. I swear a smile even crosses her lips when she looks at me. For a moment, it's like the night we met—she doesn't hate me. She might even like me a bit.

But as soon as Lina is back with the water, Tilly's expression shifts. Like a light switch, the moment is gone, and Tilly is back to glaring at me.

"Here, I'm done with the AC. I need to get back to work."

Tilly pushes the first aid kit into Lina's hands and storms off with her toolbox.

"I'm sorry about her. She's not great with change, and she's having a hard time grieving," Lina says softly.

"I didn't realize she and my aunt were so close."

"I've only lived here a few years, but from what I saw, they were very close. Benny was the mother none of us had. So just give her a little leeway right now. She's not showing her best side, but she does have one," Lina says.

I just nod, taking it all in.

A line starts to form, so Lina gets back to work, and I grab my stuff. I hold everything in my right hand, keeping my left hand free and bandaged.

I head back to my place, spotting Tilly heading toward the apple orchard. I've been down there a few times to check on things, but it's not like I really know what the apples should look like. I know they'll be ready in time for apple-picking season, but that's about it. Everyone else reassures me Tilly handles their care, and every year they're delicious.

My phone rings as I get through the front door, but it's my mother's special ringtone, so I let it go to voicemail. I learned early on that having a special ringtone for her helped avoid unnecessary conversations. Half the time she just needs someone to hear her think. But I have enough going on, and I'm not in the mood to answer questions about how selling the place is going.

I can't tell anyone the truth about this place—even if it slowly kills me. Maybe that's how Aunt Blake died. She lived with this secret and didn't even have a plan.

At least I have one outlined—even if Tilly doesn't like it. It's not like she's over here offering anything else.

Tilly

"You know what else pisses me off? Her schedules. Like, we had a perfectly good schedule in place before she came around." I sigh. Sipping another gulp of my beer, I look at my friends. Hattie and Lina both look at each other before looking back at me. "What?"

"Nothing," they say in unison—which means something is definitely up.

"Come on, what?" I sigh, setting down my beer.

"We just think you talk a lot about her, considering how much you *hate* her," Hattie says slowly.

"I mean, I'm just complaining." I frown.

"Are you? Because it seems like you're mistaking distaste for actually liking her," Lina says. She tucks her blonde hair behind her ear and waits for me to speak.

"I don't like her. Are you guys kidding?" I laugh, because they have to be messing with me right now. How could I like someone like that? Especially with all I've said.

"We just think when someone bothers you this much it's because maybe on a deeper level you actually like her," Lina says and Hattie nods.

"Well, this is great, do you often get together to talk about me?" I scoff and pick up my beer.

"You know that's not—" Hattie starts, but I cut her off.

"I need another beer." I finish mine and head for the bar instead of waiting for a bartender.

"Another beer, Til?" Bill, the bartender asks. He's your typical macho man who cares way too much about how thin a woman is and how much makeup she uses instead of how smart she is. But he can make a mean mixed drink, and he doesn't let anyone homophobic come in here. So we try to overlook his flaws.

"Nah, can you make me something stronger? I don't care what it is." I sit down at the bar and glance back at my friends. They're looking at me, pleading with their eyes for me to come back, but I hold my ground.

I've sat through their share of relationship troubles and never batted an eye. But I complain about our boss—who stole the only thing I worked my ass off for—and suddenly I'm the issue? Nah. I'm pissed. It's normal to complain about things to your friends. And it isn't like that's all I do—then I'd understand. But beer nights is, and has always been, our time to bitch about life. Suddenly that doesn't apply anymore?

Bill places a fancy looking drink in front of me. It's red and even has an umbrella in it. Without thinking twice, I toss it back. Gulping down the warm liquid, I can tell it's some sort of tequila mixed with orange juice and something else. I assume it's his take on a tequila sunrise. I place the empty glass on the bar and ask for another.

"Only if you promise not to puke. I'm not cleaning that up," he says with a chuckle.

"Deal." I nod. I can handle my liquor.

As the alcohol hits my empty stomach, I think about going back to my friends. Maybe I'm talking about Bells a little too much, and I can afford to stop. But as I turn to look at them, I see them watching the door. My eyes follow suit, and I see the auburn curls I was just complaining about, hanging down to her waist, which are covered in these tight ripped jeans. She's wearing a pair of heels that look taller than my drink glass. My friends wave her over, and she heads right toward them. What the actual fuck? Did they invite her? Did they invite her and didn't tell me?

"I'll put it on your tab. Wasn't that the chick you hooked up with a few weeks back?" Bill asks, nodding toward Bells.

"Yes," I grumble. One of the worst things about a small town is everyone knows your business. Especially the town bartender.

"Looks like she and your friends are getting along," he muses before putting another drink in front of me.

I take a long sip before picking it up and walking over to my friends. I stand behind Lina, and Bells smiles at me. Her pretty red lipstick highlights her hair and shows off her pouty lips. God, I hate how the alcohol is getting to me right now.

"Do you want to pull up a chair?" Bells asks, like she isn't intruding on my night with my friends.

"No thanks, I came to get my phone." I had left it on the table, but now I grab it and turn to go.

"Wait! Where are you going?" Lina stops me, grabbing the back of my arm.

"I'll be at the bar."

"You can join us," Hattie says.

"I'd really rather not." I scoff.

"She's not that bad when you get to know her. I thought maybe you'd be more relaxed outside of work," Lina explains.

"Is that why you invited her without telling me?" I'm probably being louder than I intend, because Bells perks up but doesn't say anything. She makes eye contact with me for a brief second before dropping it.

"I just thought it might help smooth things over." Lina sighs.

"Whatever. I'll see you guys later." I shake my head and walk back to the bar.

I sit on an old leathery stool and sip my drink. I pull out my phone, thumb hovering over the hookup app, then sigh. There was never anyone new on there—just the same guys I went to high school with or have already hooked up with. I shove the phone back into my pocket and glance at the door just as it swings open.

In strolls a bachelorette party: one woman in a white veil clipped to a rhinestone-studded cowboy hat, surrounded by her entourage in matching black shirts with snarky wedding slogans and bubblegum-pink hats. The backs of the shirts flaunt the bride's name and today's date in glittering letters.

Maybe the pickings tonight won't be so slim after all.

"Bartender! Can we get lots of shots?!" a busty blonde says, and Bill nods, staring directly at her tits. I knew they were out there, but he didn't have to be so obvious about it. She puts down a credit card, asking for an open tab, and walks away.

"Lemme take them over," I tell Bill as the group heads toward the back of the bar.

"What?" He looks at me like I have ten heads.

"Come on, I'm trying to score. Let me take them over, and I'll bring back the tip," I offer.

"Fine, but if you drop 'em you pay for 'em." He waits for me to accept and then starts pouring the shots.

I take the tray over to the group, and they're devoured by the second. I'm not sure who's into women yet, but I figure at least one of them has to be. Or maybe one is at least curious about being with a woman. I love a bi-curious woman.

"I'm Tilly, anyone wanna help me get some more shots?" I switch into flirt mode, glancing around the circle of beautiful women. The busty blonde jumps up, her tits almost knocking her friend over.

"I'll help!" It's clear they've all already been drinking tonight, but no one is more drunk than I am. And I'm in a very happy, tipsy space.

"A beautiful woman helping me, I must know your name." I wink at her, and she turns pink.

"Sophie."

"Well, Sophie. Are y'all from around here?" I ask, already knowing the answer. They're renting an Airbnb nearby, and their pregnant friend drove them over.

"Nah, we're from the city but wanted a weekend away." Sophie smiles.

"Well, have you ever been up here before?"

"No, but it's so nice. We'll definitely be coming back sometime."

"Well, Sophie, I might just have to convince you to try something else new tonight." I wink again, and this time she giggles.

"What's that?" She leans in closer, her breasts almost escaping her low-cut top.

"Why don't we get your friends their drinks, and then I'll show you?" I suggest as we reach the bar. Bill is looking at me with envy because Sophie can't take her eyes off me.

"Sounds good."

We bring the shots over. This time I take one, then take Sophie's hand. I press a few buttons on the old jukebox the bar has hooked up. It doesn't use coins anymore but plays whatever people want. I pick an old song with a good beat and catch Bells looking at me as I lead Sophie to the makeshift dance floor. I spin Sophie around a few times, then pull her in close so our bodies are touching while we dance. Out of the corner of my eye, I see Bells watching. I can't help it—it's like my eyes are magnets to her. I'm dancing with Sophie, and all I see is Bells.

Her beautiful curls cascade down her body like a waterfall, her curves teasing me in her achingly tight clothes. She pulls her beer to her lips, and I watch her lips wrap around the opening of the bottle. Fuck, what I wouldn't do to have those lips on me again. I spin Sophie around, and Bells bites down on her bottom lip. Flipping her hair, she goes back to talking to my friends, and I internally growl. Does she have to take everything from me? Yeah, I know she isn't literally stealing my friends, and maybe I'm childish, but I don't want to share them tonight.

The song is about to end, but just as it does, Sophie pulls me in for a kiss. For a moment, I'm so surprised that my eyes are wide open as she plants her lips on mine. She sort of licks my lips and is more chewing my face than actually kissing. Is it possible that this woman is a bit more intoxicated than I thought? All I know is there's definitely no way I'd bring her home. If she's this bad of a kisser, I can't even imagine how bad the sex would be. I have a feeling she'd be worse than my yearly pap smear. I attempt to pull away from her, but she doesn't get the hint and keeps kissing me.

"Babe?! I leave for the bathroom and you're kissing someone else?!" Bells appears in front of us, yelling. My eyes go wide in confusion, but Bells winks, and I realize this is her attempt at saving me.

"Is this your girlfriend?!" Sophie gasps.

"I'm her fiancée! We just got engaged last night, and just because the ring didn't fit doesn't mean you can go kissing other women!" Bells turns on the theatrics, and Sophie is eating this up.

"I'm so sorry." I hang my head in shame.

"I'm the one who kissed her. She asked me to dance, but I'm so sorry," Sophie starts apologizing, but Bells holds up her hand.

"Can you just go? I think my fiancée and I need to talk this out. Who knows if there will even be a wedding after this!" Bells waves Sophie off, who runs toward her friends at full speed and Bells pulls me outside.

"Holy shit. You were scary good in there," I say in awe.

"I could tell you needed a save and your friends were worried they wouldn't be believable enough." She shrugs.

"You could tell I needed help?"

"She looked like she was trying to lick something off your face, and you had pure terror in your very OPEN eyes." Bells laughs. "I just figured you could use an easy out." She shrugs.

"Thanks." I smile.

"Plus, I knew you wouldn't be taking her home if that's how she kissed. So how else would you get out of that?" She winks. She remembered I said that the night we met? Maybe she wasn't as terrible as I originally thought.

ELEVEN

Bells

Tilly is the first thing on my mind when I wake up. Well, actually she's the second, after the stinging hangover headache. But that's her fault too for recommending those tequila sunrise drinks Bill kept making. After our little performance, I had to pretend to be Tilly's fiancée all night, so we sat together and drank with her friends. It's nice seeing a different side of her—the side I might have gotten to know if Aunt Blake had left her the orchard instead of me. She has this amazing smile that I try committing to memory, just in case last night was a case of beer goggles.

I get out of bed, head for the bathroom, and grab the bottle of Motrin. I take two pills while I pee before I jump in the shower. My makeup from last night is smudged on my face, and my hair is a tangled mess. Today is my day off from the orchard and from my actual job, so I have time to take a relaxing shower. I turn up the heat and let it get all steamy. By the time I come out, all the mirrors are fogged, and I feel like a new person. I change into comfy clothes and make a fresh cup of coffee.

Standing on my back porch in my slippers, I overlook the orchard. It's more crowded today, and everyone has my number if they need me, but I suspect they won't. From what I've learned, this place is a well-oiled machine. Everyone knows what they're doing and where they should be. It's still not anywhere near capacity or where I'd like it to be. I'm hoping to introduce some of the new ideas on Monday along with the new website. I know there's going to be some pushback at first, especially from Tilly, but I'm hoping she understands.

Finishing my coffee, I decide to tackle the one thing I've been putting off—going through Aunt Blake's bedroom. Most of the house I've already cleaned out of anything unnecessary, all the medical equipment was donated, and I've gotten my stuff moved in. Bracing myself and grabbing garbage bags and boxes on the way, I head for Aunt Blake's bedroom. It's a bit of a mess; it seems like someone was looking for something and was in a rush. I wonder if that was Aunt Blake or someone who took care of her while she was sick.

Starting small, I open her bedside table. It's full of random notes, none of which I can make out, but they're definitely in her handwriting. I'm just glad I don't find a box of condoms or something. I don't think I'd want to find that. Under the bed is next, which is of course filled with dust—mostly old shoes, dust bunnies, and a few pieces of clothes that must have gotten kicked under there by mistake. I toss all the clothes and shoes into boxes for donation. Everything is a little dusty but otherwise in great condition.

In the top drawer of her dresser, I find three envelopes, each one addressed to Tilly, Hattie, and Lina. They aren't sealed, so I open them just to scan them, maybe to find some indication why she chose me as the orchard heir. Lina and Hattie's are harmless, even kind, but it's Tilly's that gives me pause. She explains why she didn't leave the orchard to Tilly and how it's failing. Apparently, my aunt had been keeping track of me and what I'd been doing with my life. She had faith that I could turn things around for everyone. And if I couldn't, at least Tilly wouldn't be stuck in a field of debt or having to claim bankruptcy. It's kind, and it makes a lot of sense, but I can't give her this yet. If I give her this, she'll learn the truth about the orchard's status, and there's no sense in making her worry more than I already am. I take the three letters and bring them to my room, tucking them into the bottom drawer of my dresser. Once I figure things out either way, I'll give them all the notes.

The rest of the room is fairly easy to clean out. I still don't want to sleep in there; it feels too much like being in someone else's space. At least it's cleaned out, and I know the local donation shop is happy for all these clothes and items. I'll have to call them again to collect the rest this week.

Grabbing the stack of papers I printed, I start hanging them up in the office. I'm narrowing down which things would be the least costly but bring in the biggest audience. The office is already cleaned out of Aunt Blake's stuff, so I've turned it into my own. My desk is a mess between the actual work I'm doing for the nonprofit and the budget for the orchard. The wall above my desk is covered in ideas either on Post-its or printer paper. I need to finalize everything today so we can have whatever we need ordered by the fall season, which apparently starts at the end of August. I think that's too hot for people to be visiting, but according to the staff, they come in their fall attire and buy apples, eat apple-cider donuts, and take the hayrides.

So far, I have the basics. There's going to be more of a focus on things we can advertise online. I'm sticking with setting up the influencer days, but I also want to focus on family activities and maybe a few date-night-themed activities. Some of them include outsourcing things like a DJ for a line-dancing night and a bartender for a bar night with apple-cider flights. But others, like the masquerade dance, don't need too much except for decorations.

What I'm most excited about is pairing with the Sapphire Falls library, where all the locals who have or open a library card get free apple-picking admission and discounted tickets. It's something I hope will bring in more of the local community, like Tilly wants. I've also contacted my friends in the city and managed to get a discount on Metro-North tickets for anyone visiting the orchard for an event. By bringing in city people—as Tilly calls them—we'll be able to increase our sales. Maybe the locals aren't the ones with social media, but everyone in the city loves posting about whatever they're doing and bragging about where they went. All it takes is a few aesthetic photos or videos to go viral, and we'll be crawling with people.

I'll have to sell it to Tilly. I know I don't need her permission to do anything, but I like having her on board. Now that I know how close she and my aunt were, it feels like I'm getting my aunt's approval if I get hers. Of course, I've always been someone to have unrealistic expectations. I'm typing up the final calendar of events for the fall when I hear someone knocking at my door.

"Who is it?" I call out.

"Lina!" she shouts cheerfully. I open the front door and find the beautiful blonde on my porch.

"What's up?" I'm not really dressed for company. I pull my robe closed over my very short shorts.

"I made some new things I'd like to sell at the bakery. I used to have Benny try everything before I officially put it on the menu and wasn't sure if you'd like to do the same." She smiles, holding a wrapped tray that smells divine.

"Come on in. I'm just working on things for the orchard." I step aside.

"Do you want a moment to change? I should've called first."

"Actually yes. Do you know where the office is? Can you meet me in there?" I suggest.

"Yes." She nods and follows me up the stairs.

I head into my bedroom and change into a nice blouse and a pair of work pants. I like to feel more put-together than I look. I toss my hair in a ponytail and meet Lina in the office. She's looking over the stuff I have taped to the wall, and I can't tell if she's happy or not. She's someone who's often hard to read. She looks like a tattooed Barbie doll, busty and blonde, but she's one of the most relaxed people I know. She's often a little stoned—I learned last night she prefers that to drinking—but she's not like a typical stoner. I like picking her brain about things, so I'm curious what she thinks and if she might be able to give me advice on working with Tilly.

I was surprised when Lina and Hattie asked me to join them at the bar last night, because I know it's something they do with Tilly. But then, when Tilly was pissed at me, I could tell it was an ambush. I couldn't tell if they were tired of our fighting or just trying to force us to get along. Not that I have a problem with Tilly, but it's obvious she has one with me. I hope I win a few points with her for saving her last night. She looked like she was being tortured by that woman, and after a few minutes of enjoying it—I mean, she was obviously trying to make me jealous—I knew I had to step in.

"B, this is amazing." Lina smiles.

"Really?"

"You really paired up with the library?"

"Oh, yeah. I had a meeting with the board of directors. I figured they'd be happy because the more cards they open, the more funding they can receive," I explain.

"Wow. Tilly will love this. Have you told her yet?"

"No. I was actually hoping to get your advice on that. I know she's not thrilled with anything I do. And last time I brought up the changes, she was less than accepting." I sigh.

"She's a tough nut to crack. She and I butted heads when I first got here. She's protective and hates change. But I think she'll be more receptive since she knows you're doing all you can to keep this place going and not sell it." She smiles, and my stomach lurches. My mother's voice in the back of my head asking me about the sale of this place makes me feel like a fraud. I still haven't gained the courage to tell her I can't sell this place.

"So, these have weed in them. But I also brought some that don't have any weed in them so you can get the list," she explains. I'm a little wary about her selling edibles, but they have all the proper paperwork filled out, and it's completely legal. Lina clearly labels everything and checks ID with an actual scanner to prevent fakes from slipping through.

"I'll take the weed-free ones today. I have a bit more work to get through after this." I giggle.

"Okay, then we have the apple-cinnamon bun, the pumpkin croissant, and the pumpkin-cheesecake cinnamon bun." She points at the plate, and I pick the apple one.

Biting against the flaky, icing-covered side, I break a piece off and it melts in my mouth. Holy shit, this is amazing. I can taste the apple filling, but it's nice and warm. Along with the icing, it's sweet as hell. I take another bite, and all I want is a nice cup of hot coffee to go with it. It feels like fall in my mouth.

"Fuck, that's so good. Do you create your own recipes?"

"I do. Sometimes I choose a few I find and just combine them, but these I created," she says proudly.

"I'm going to need you to put this in the bakery for sure. Let me try the others." I reach for another pastry and wonder how I can convince her to bring me one daily.

TWELVE

Tilly

"So, you work at an apple orchard? What's that like?" the woman across from me asks.

She's beautiful, with long brown hair and a symmetrical face with minimal makeup. She just moved to town, and we met at the supermarket, talking about apples of all things. When she asked me out, I wasn't surprised, but I shocked myself by saying yes. It has been months since I've been on an actual date. The last time I even kissed a woman was that fiasco with the busty blonde at the bar. I'd been too busy at the orchard, trying to get all the new things Bells was implementing ready for the fall season.

"I like it a lot, I'm excited for the upcoming season. There's a lot of new events going on." I smile while I poke at the salmon I'm eating.

"Oh? Like what?" She's genuinely interested in what I have to say.

"We're going to add a lot of family activities for during the week and early weekends but also new events for adults after we close. We have our first wedding booked and we're trying to have a masquerade night as well." It probably sounded like I was bragging, which was ironic with the way I first reacted about these ideas.

"Wow, I've never heard of so much going on at an orchard."

"They were my boss' ideas. She inherited the orchard a few months ago and decided to shake things up. I wasn't fully on board when she suggested them. But honestly, I'm impressed by how she pulled them off." Not that I'd say that to her. I don't want to see the smug look on her face.

"I'll have to check it out. It sounds like a good time."

"Yeah, my boss pulled all of it together in less than three months which is like almost unheard of. Apparently, she had a lot of contacts in the city; that's where she's originally from, and they helped a lot. It's all coming together, and we have the start of the season opening next week." I smile.

"What else do you do?" she asks.

"Well, lately all my focus is building things for the opening. Bells has me fixing all the signage, painting and of course taking care of the animals on the farm—"

"I meant, what else do you do outside of the farm?" she asks politely.

"Oh, well not much these days. Sometimes my friends and Bells go to the local bar in town, but even on those nights we can't help but talk about work. She's kind of a hard worker, but she really wants this place to succeed. It's admirable." I smile.

My date, Jenna purses her lips and pauses before waving the waiter over. "Can we have the check please?" The waiter nods, and I look at her surprised. We haven't had dessert, and she is already done?

"Did I say something wrong?"

"It's obvious you're in love with this boss of yours. So I'm not quite sure why you're here tonight. But I don't wish to be in the middle of some drama I can't win." She uses her napkin to wipe the corners of her mouth as I process what she's saying.

"I'm not in love with my boss," I say quietly.

"Look, it's fine. Maybe you haven't admitted it to yourself yet, but you clearly have feelings for her you need to work out." She pulls out her credit card and places it on the table for the waiter.

"But I don't—"

"If you weren't in love with her there's no way you'd go on and on about her. I know more about her after today than I do about you. And that's fine, it's just not what I'm looking for. For what it's worth, I hope you get her. She sounds great." She smiles and takes off after signing the receipt.

I sit there in silence. Have I just been dumped mid-date? I push back my plate and head for the door. I'm not in the mood to finish eating and I need to get out of here. If no one overheard what just happened, I don't need the town speculating with me sitting alone. Heading for my truck, I grip the steering wheel when I get in.

Why was everyone so insistent that there was something going on between Bells and me? Sure, we don't hate each other as much as we used to. I got over that when I realized she was working hard to save this place. She wants to bring new people in and that means she isn't going to be selling anytime soon. Why would she fix it up just to sell it? But that doesn't mean I'm in love with her. I just like her as a boss. Or an acquaintance of sorts. She isn't as bad as I originally thought, but it isn't like that negates everything.

The drive home is quicker than I wish, and I'm pulling into my driveway. Hattie and Lina are busy tonight—Lina's trying new recipes, which means she's either stoned or cooking, and Hattie is having a movie night in with Ollie. I could probably join them, and they wouldn't mind, but I don't want to feel like an intruder. I head toward my front door when I hear an alarm going off. It's a consistent beeping that I can only make out a bit. I grab the bat I keep in the back of my truck and head toward the sound. It isn't coming from my house, so I follow it toward the barn. Is someone trying to break into the horses? We have a pretty low-key system considering we live in the middle of nowhere, and it would take a lot to get on this road undetected. But I wasn't home, so maybe someone did pass through?

Quietly, I creep toward the barn and confirm my suspicions. The beeping is louder, and I hear someone muttering under their breath, trying to shut it off. There's a variety of beeps from the system as they try to guess the code, and I push the door open quickly, holding up the bat in case they're bigger than me.

"Holy fuck!" Bells screams and jumps down to the ground.

"What the hell are you doing?" I put the bat down and turn off the alarm with the correct code.

"I'm sorry. I heard a weird noise and wanted to check it out." She frowns, standing up and dusting the dirt off her pants.

"What noise?" I raise an eyebrow.

"It sounded like a raccoon, and I thought maybe it got stuck in here or something, so I thought I should check it out. I knocked on your door first, but you weren't home." She glances over my outfit, probably able to tell that I was on a date.

"Where was the noise coming from?"

"Toward the side." She points, and I do hear a sound, but it doesn't sound like a raccoon. They know the food isn't in here—they usually raid the dumpster behind Lina's bakery.

"It's a chipmunk, and it looks like he's got a hurt paw." The chipmunk is lying on the floor in the corner, licking one of its legs and making a sound like whimpers. "Can you bring me that blanket?" I point to the small blanket in the front of the barn.

Bells brings it over, and I carefully walk toward the chipmunk. It looks terrified, but I scoop it into the blanket and hold it so it isn't trapped. I don't want it to feel like I'm attacking it.

"I'm going to bring you to someone who can help," I tell the little thing.

"Hattie can fix chipmunks?" Bells looks on in confusion.

"She can help most animals. It's not the first time we've come across hurt wildlife. We try to do what we can," I explain.

"I see." Bells follows me out of the barn, locking up behind me. We head toward Hattie's house, and she knocks on the front door.

"Hey, we found this little one in the barn. Can you help?" I look up at Hattie, who waves us inside.

"Ollie! Go get my medical bag!" she calls out and leads us into her office.

One of the rooms in her house has been made into a makeshift office. Every once in a while, she gets someone local needing help with their pet, and we try whatever we can. So she has all these veterinarian supplies and furniture in her office. I place the blanket and chipmunk on the table and hold my hands cautiously nearby in case it tries to escape—not that I think that's possible. Ollie runs in with her bag of supplies, and she takes out a bunch of different things.

"It's possible there will be some blood—you might want to wait in the other room," I say, turning toward Bells. I don't want her becoming the next patient on the table.

She nods and smiles. "Thank you."

"Ollie, can you go sit with her? I think she could use a friend," I ask him. He smiles proudly, probably happy to have a grown-up job.

"Will he be okay?" I ask Hattie quietly.

"Yeah. It just looks like a bite from another animal that isn't healing right. I'm going to clean it out and then wrap it. I'd like to keep him inside for about a week or so, but it'll really depend on him," she says, looking at the chipmunk.

"Bells is the one who found him. She set the alarm on the barn off looking for him," I say.

"She didn't strike me as an animal lover." Hattie raises an eyebrow.

"She continues to surprise me." I glance over to where she's laughing with Ollie in the living room. He's showing her one of his animal books, and she's asking questions about whatever he's saying.

"How'd your date tonight go?" Hattie asks, breaking my thoughts.

"Oh, not great." I sigh.

"Care to elaborate?" She's cleaning the chipmunk's cut, and I'm making sure he doesn't try to run away.

"She left early. For some reason she's under the impression that I'm harboring feelings for Bells," I say quietly.

"No way. Really?" Hattie's voice is heavy with sarcasm.

"What is up with that? Why does everyone keep doing that to me?" I groan.

"Because it's so obvious you're into her." She laughs.

"Just because I no longer hate her doesn't mean I'm in love with her or something." I scoff.

"I mean, no. But you do. It's obvious in your interactions and the way you look at her."

"I know she's beautiful—that's why I hooked up with her that first night. But it's not like I think about that anymore. It was a one-time thing before I knew who she was."

"But now that you know she isn't who you originally thought she was, hasn't your view on her softened?" Hattie asks.

"Yeah, but not enough to say I'm into her."

"Okay." Hattie makes a face but drops the conversation.

Hattie finishes taking care of the chipmunk and calls Ollie and Bells back in. His little leg is wrapped up, and she's finding an old shoebox to keep him in for the week. She and Ollie have a habit of taking in strays and nursing them back to health, so it isn't abnormal for them.

"The little guy needs a name," Bells says, looking at him.

"You should name him—you found him," Ollie says.

"That's true." I nod.

"How about Peanut?" She smiles.

"That's funny. Can we feed him peanuts?" Ollie asks.

"We can. Actually, we should get him some food. I don't know how long it's been since his last meal," Hattie says. She and Ollie head for the kitchen, and I look at Bells.

"Thanks for taking him here—and not hitting me with that baseball bat. Now I know never to sneak up on you," she teases.

"Thanks for trying to save him. The code is 1919, by the way, in case you ever need it again."

"Good to know, just in case I need to save any more chipmunks." She laughs.

THIRTEEN

Bells

We only have two weeks before the season here starts. Our first huge event is on the fifteenth of August, and it starts at ten a.m. but goes all the way into the night. We have family activities planned all day and then at night we have fireworks and adult activities. I hired three new workers for the season to help out at the front gate for admission, someone to help Lina in the bakery, and a cashier. I was nervous about it all coming together in time. Tilly gave me some pushback, but now that it's been a few months, she seems to be coming around.

Tomorrow is what I'm most worried about—influencer day. We'll have almost one hundred influencers from all over the tri-state area visiting and agreeing to make content for waived admission. We have the day planned for lots of photo activities, including an old photo booth I've talked the town into letting us borrow for the day. Our focus is to get them through the orchard, showing the beauty, trying all of Lina's delicious treats, and seeing the animals. If it works, it means tons of posts about the orchard with their agreement to post a few times throughout the season. Tilly still thinks it's a waste of time—something I can't seem to change her opinion on—but I'm willing to risk it. I've seen businesses thrive after one viral video, so it can't hurt to create that.

Besides, it's all we can do. If the orchard doesn't make any money this month, I have to shut down by September first. I have talked all the vendors into extending our bills. They knew Benny and see how hard I'm working to get this place back up and running the way she had. But they still need to be paid, and I know I can't hold them off much longer. It's the true test of how hard I've worked the last several months.

"Tilly! Can you help me?" I call to her from across the field.

"What's up?" She jogs over in those overalls that make me forget how to talk to her.

"I don't like the way the hay looks on this, but I underestimated how heavy these hay bales are. Can you help?" I hate asking for help, but they aren't as light as I thought they were.

"You don't like the way the hay looks?" She smirks, like she's trying to hold back laughter.

"I want to create a vibe up here, but right now it looks messy and thrown together."

"Because it's hay…" she says, deadpan.

"Yes, but we want to create an experience. If it doesn't look good, they might not mention it in their content."

"So?" She winces, and I sigh.

"We want them to mention as many of our opportunities as possible. Maybe there are followers who are specifically looking for a fun hayride. We don't want to miss out on that because of a mess," I explain.

"That sounds ridiculous."

"I didn't ask. Can you help me or not?" I put my hands on my hips and raise an eyebrow at her.

"Yeah." She mumbles and grabs a barrel of hay before climbing up on the trailer.

"Okay, so I want it right over there. They need to be more evenly distributed, with enough space for people to find a seat, but also for one line in the middle for extra seats." I explain my vision.

"You're going to need to sweep if you don't want people falling," she says as she starts rearranging the hay.

"I know." I lean over the side of the trailer and reach for the broom. I'm pulling it up over the side when my footing starts to slip, and I'm about to fall over the edge when I feel an arm pull me back.

"You really are dangerous. I hope we have good insurance," Tilly jokes as she looks at me. I'm in her arms, one hand holding the broom, the other around her. She carefully helps me stand, and I blush.

"Thanks." She nods and goes back to the other side of the trailer as I begin to sweep.

We keep having moments like this, where we brush hands or touch and I think it's something, and she goes back to ignoring me. I guess it's an improvement from being pissed at me, but I hate playing games. It isn't like I want anything from her—we're coworkers—and I'm fine with that.

"Did you see Peanut today?" I ask.

"Yes. Hattie says he's doing well and eating, so that's a good sign," she says.

"Good." It's an awkward pause as I finish sweeping and she moves around the hay.

"B! Come quick! We need you!" Lina calls from the doorway of her bakery.

I look at Tilly, but she's already following. If it isn't something I can fix, Tilly usually can.

"What's going on?" I ask as we get inside.

"The AC stopped working, and it blew out the electricity in here. The ovens aren't working; neither are the registers or anything," Lina says, panicking.

"Like you need Tilly to fix it again?" I ask hopefully.

"No, this has never happened before," Lina says.

"If the AC blew the electricity, that's not something I can fix.

That's something an electrician needs to come check out. If there's a wire or something broken and I only fix the AC, I could start an electrical fire," Tilly explains.

'Oh' is all I can say, because of course it happens today, the day before opening. "Do we know a local electrician?"

"We've never had to call one, but I'm sure we can find one," Tilly says.

"And what if they can't fix it today?" I ask.

"Then I can't cook anything, and we have no snacks for tomorrow," Lina says quietly.

"Okay. Okay," I just keep saying, because my brain is in overdrive trying to think of anything I can possibly do to fix it.

"Look, I'll handle this. You go take care of everything else. I'll make this my priority and do what I can," Tilly says.

"Are you sure?" I ask.

"Yes. We shouldn't both freak out about this, so let's just see what I can do, and you finish up whatever's on your checklist." She smiles, squeezing the sides of my shoulders.

"How do you know I have a checklist?" I crack a smile.

"Because you have one for everything. So go do that, and I'll text you with updates," Tilly says.

"Okay." I pause. "Lina, the oven at my house is big enough to bake a lot, right? Can you cook there?"

"Oh my gosh, it is!" Lina's eyes light up.

"Okay, gather whoever you need and have them help you bring supplies over. Cook the essentials and things that are most photographical. Things that are also easy to transport for when we fix this. Here are my keys." I toss her my keychain, and she runs outside to get help.

I take a deep breath before opening my phone to look over my checklist. I'm impressed by how easily Tilly handles that. She's going to take care of this issue, and I have to set up the photo booth, the signs by the entrance, and put the wooden baskets for apples at the end of each row of apple trees. We figure if not for photos, it will be a cute way for people to carry apples back to the store. Thank God Tilly is taking over, because I'm so anxious about tomorrow I can't think straight. Just knowing it's in her hands is such a relief.

She has become someone I can rely on. No matter what it is, if it's something she can help with, she's there. I can see why my aunt thought so highly of her. She's dependable, just like her friends said. Even if it will take some time, I know I'll be doing my best to break in and knock down that wall she has for me.

"Um, Bells?" One of the apple helpers taps on my shoulder.

"Yes?" I force a smile and try to focus on them.

"We have a little issue with the decorations for tomorrow." She winces like she's afraid of my reaction.

"What kind of issue?" I ask patiently.

"It seems like the printer mixed things up, and instead of Sapphire Falls Orchard, it says Sapphic Falls Orchard." She holds out her phone to show me the sign unfolded.

"Shit. Do we have the printer's number?" We used a big company to save some money but now look at us.

"We do, but they can't get a new sign until next week," she explains.

"Okay." I pause, trying to think of any options we might have. A few deep breaths do nothing for the anxiety I'm having.

"What's going on?" Tilly walks over. The worker whose name I should really know explains the situation, and Tilly studies me. I'm sure she's thinking I'm such a fuckup for not double-checking all the signage before the event. It's completely on me.

"There's a print shop just out of town. Take the truck and head there now. I'll text you the correct images for the banner, and do not leave until you have it in your hand. Understood?" Tilly instructs the woman, who nods before accepting Tilly's keys.

"Will they be able to help?" I don't know what time it is, but it's cutting things close.

"I believe so, but, hey, if not, we have more than enough

signs. And maybe they'll think the sign is cute or on purpose. We can save it for a sapphic event; that way it doesn't go to waste," Tilly suggests with a smile.

"Wow," I say aloud.

"What?" She looks confused.

"I don't know how you do that."

"Do what?" She frowns.

"I'm freaking out and everything seems to be going wrong, but you swoop in and save the day. It's like you know exactly what to do and what to say," I admit.

"I've just been here a long time. Things happen, and you have to be able to roll with the punches. By the way, we have the electrician coming in the next hour, and, depending on how that goes, we'll know more about tomorrow. Don't worry, little lamb," Tilly says with a wink.

"Thanks." I blush.

Tilly studies my face for a moment before reaching for my face. She touches my hair, her fingers twirling one of my curls. I close my eyes, thinking she's about to lean in and kiss me. But instead, she pulls on my curl, and in her hand is a loose piece of hay. She drops it to the ground, winks at me, and heads back for the bakery. What the hell was that? I think we're having a moment, and it feels like it's all in my head. I hate how she has this effect on me. I can't continue on with her like this. I feel myself slowly going crazy, wondering if it's all in my head.

I think it is, and then her friends allude to her feelings, and I go questioning myself all over again. They've not-so-subtly been pushing us toward each other for months now. It wasn't so obvious at first—always inviting me out. But now they insist on us talking alone, driving places together, and leaving when we're in the same room. I can't tell if they're putting themselves up to it or Tilly has said something. But I guess if she has, then by now she knows I'm interested enough for her to make some kind of move. I think my flirting back has been obvious, even if I'm not sure how I feel.

FOURTEEN

Tilly

The school buses pull in exactly at noon. Bells has arranged for all the guests to be picked up at the train station and brought here on the local school buses. It's a cheap arrangement for us, and then no one needs to worry about transportation. As the people pile in, I'm amazed at the diversity—not just in looks, but in gender and age. She has managed to hit almost every group of people and get them here. The second they get off the bus, they pull out their phones and record everything. I have a feeling I'm in the background of a lot of TikToks right now.

Bells makes a little speech as we hand out maps of the orchard—newly improved maps with the new logo, links to our social media pages, and the new website. As much as I hate to admit it, the improvements to our social pages and website are amazing. It looks more cohesive and is very user-friendly. There are fewer phone calls to the main office because there's even a frequently asked questions page on the site. All the people disperse, and I head to the barn to keep an eye on the horses. No one is allowed to ride them this weekend, so I want to make sure no one tries.

"Have you seen that hot-ass blondie? I heard there's a masc shortage, but God damn," one woman whispers.

"Tell me about it. I'd like to climb her like a tree, if you know what I mean," the other says, and they both giggle.

I smirk to myself. It isn't the first time I've been ogled. But it's the first time it's happened while Bells is in earshot. I don't know why, but it makes me happy that she knows how people lust over me. It isn't like I'm going to fuck some influencer, but I like being admired. I mean, who doesn't?

"You look happy. You doing okay?" Hattie asks, sneaking up behind me.

"Just taking this all in. It's more people than I expected," I admit.

"Bells said it was at least one hundred."

"I know, but I didn't think they'd all show up. It's kind of impressive," I say.

"Have you told her that?" Hattie raises an eyebrow.

"No. She doesn't need me telling her she's doing a good job." I scoff.

"It doesn't hurt to hear a compliment sometimes. Especially when it's a new job and the person you work with has been an ass in the past," Hattie says.

"I've been better!"

"You have. But it wouldn't hurt for you to tell her she did a good job. You can admit that she surprised you." Hattie smiles.

"She has. I really thought she was going to turn this place up for profit. I mean, she still could." I shrug.

"She's not like that. She's worked so hard to make this place even better than it was before without getting rid of its core. I know you two had a rocky start, but isn't it time you put that in the past? Kiss and make up and all that?"

"Oh yeah? Kiss and make up? You sound like Lina." I roll my eyes.

"We just want you to be happy. And you may not see it, but we see how she lights you up."

"This isn't weird for you?" I frown. We don't talk much about me seeing someone since she told me she had feelings for me. I don't want to make her uncomfortable.

"No, I thought it might be. At first it wasn't great, but then I realized all I want is for you to be happy. Even if that isn't with me, you deserve someone who makes you smile."

"And this is why you're my best friend." I pull her in for a tight hug.

"Excuse me!? I'm in the bakery for one day and you replace me?" Lina teases, walking into the barn.

"What are you doing here?" I laugh.

"I thought you were working the bakery?" Hattie says, confused. The electrician pulled a miracle, and since there was just an old fuse blown, he was able to repair it rather quickly. The bill was insane, but we'll make it all back in a day or so.

"I just came to bring you both some breakfast. Treats are going quickly, so I wanted to make sure you both ate." She hands us each a brown paper bag. I can smell the cinnamon and apples, making me hope it's one of the apple turnovers I love.

"Thank you," Hattie and I say in unison.

"Of course. Come see me later. I gotta get back." She hurries off toward the bakery, and we open the bags. Sure enough, inside is a warm apple turnover covered in cinnamon sugar.

I take a bite and moan. Hattie's eyes flutter to mine, but quickly catching herself, she looks away. I don't mean for it to sound sexual, but holy shit it's good. Everything Lina makes is good, but these are my favorite. If I don't have an energy drink this morning, I might follow her back to the bakery for a fresh cup of coffee. Hattie takes a bite of her pumpkin scone, and I make a face. I am not a pumpkin spice person. I don't understand how people call it pumpkin spice when there's never any real pumpkin in it. Half the time it's the taste of nutmeg. Plus, I don't care for the taste. But Hattie loves it; she drinks pumpkin-flavored coffee year-round.

"Tilly? Can you help me with something?" Bells's voice startles me from my thoughts.

I nod, unable to speak with the turnover in my mouth. Finishing the last bite, I follow quickly behind her. She's walking faster than normal, so I can tell she needs me to keep up. When I can speak without choking, I ask what's up.

"I totally forgot about the gift bags we're giving out, and I need help getting them out of the storage closet. Can you help?"

"Of course." I nod. She looks nervous, which makes sense. A lot is riding on her today.

"Okay, it's in here, but they're on the top shelf, and they're too heavy for me to lift over my head." She frowns, and we both step into the walk-in closet in the main building. It's where we sell tickets and where the bathrooms are, so right now it's fairly empty. I step into the closet behind Bells as she flicks on the light and points out the boxes. I reach for the two boxes and put them on the floor. They're a little heavy, so I'll only be able to take one at a time, but it should be fine.

"Can you get the door?" I ask Bells as I pick up the first box.

"Sure." Bells nods, but when she twists the door handle, it doesn't move. "What the…"

"Is it jammed?" I put down the box to investigate.

"It's not opening," Bells says in a voice clearly trying not to panic.

I twist the handle myself, and sure enough, it isn't budging. It must lock automatically from the outside, and we are trapped. I don't know how to tell Bells that without her freaking out.

"We seem to be trapped, but we can call Hattie, and she'll have us out in a moment," I say. Maybe providing her with the solution along with the problem will help.

"Sure." Bells nods, but I can tell by the look on her face and her wide eyes that she's still freaking out.

I pull out my phone to call Hattie, but I have no service. I try anyway, hoping it'll magically connect, but it doesn't even let the phone ring. Shit. Now I really don't have good news. I try texting her instead, hoping by some miracle that it will send.

"Do you have service?" I ask quietly.

Bells' eyes widen, and she pulls out her phone. "No."

"Okay, well, I tried texting Hattie, but until we have service there's not much we can do. I'm sure Hattie will come get us eventually." I try to reassure her.

Bells starts breathing heavily, and before she has a panic attack and passes out in here, I grab her hand. After helping her sit down on the stack of boxes, she looks at me, and I try to think of something calming to say.

"I think you do a really good job with the event today."

Bells laughs. "Ha! You didn't even want it to happen."

"I know, and that's why it kills me to even admit that. But if this many people can show up for a free day, imagine who will show up when we have some big events going on."

"I tried telling you that." She cracks a smile. I take a seat across from her, not letting go of her hand.

"I know, but sometimes I have a hard time seeing what's in front of me," I admit.

Bells pauses, and I can feel the tension between us. It's as raw and tight as it was the night we met. Her cherry-red lips are begging to be kissed. Her hand wraps around mine tightly, and we don't break eye contact. Her hazels warm to my own as I smile. Maybe my friends are right—maybe she isn't so bad. And maybe there's something between us after all. Because in this moment, the only thing I want to do is lean in and kiss her. Maybe fuck her against the wall and have her begging me to cum.

She stares at my lips and then back at my eyes. Her breathing is steady again, nowhere near nervous territory anymore. Meanwhile, I can feel my own heart beating out of my chest. She's lighting a fire in me I'm not sure I want put out. For months I've thought that fire is because I'm angry for Benny leaving her the orchard. But maybe I've mistaken that fire that is so clearly desire for anger. Now that the anger is gone, I can see Bells in a whole new light.

I lean in, just an inch, to see if this is what she wants. I don't want to try to kiss her and have her slap me or something. But she moves closer too, her lips pouty and perfect. I reach up, pushing some of her curls out of her face. Then I leave my hand there, holding her chin, and gaze into her eyes.

RING! RING! RING!

My phone rings, jolting the two of us apart. I jump up and answer the call.

"Tills? Where are you? I need help!" Hattie says from the other end.

"Hattie! We're stuck in the storage closet at the main building! Come quick, please!" I say as quickly as I possibly can. I don't know how long I'll have service or if it'll cut out.

"We? Who's with—" The phone cuts out.

"Hattie? Hattie?" I say, but it's no use. My phone says call failed, and she's gone.

"Was that Hattie?" Bells asks quietly.

"Yes. She should be on her way," I say.

"Good. We have a lot to do." Bells' cheeks are as red as her lips, and she avoids eye contact with me. Gone is our moment, gone is feeling like there are no other cares in the world.

Fifteen minutes later, Hattie is there with the backup set of keys to let us out. Bells takes off as soon as the door opens, and I'm left moving boxes with Hattie. She looks at me quizzically, but I guess she can read my mood well enough to know I don't want to talk. I don't know what I'm feeling, and I don't want to think about it right now.

FIFTEEN

Bells

Influencer day is finally over, everyone is on the train home, and we're already getting so many notifications and followers that I have to turn off my notifications. The rest of the day went okay; things went wrong but it was nothing Tilly and I couldn't fix. We made a good team, both of us putting out fires all day long. The one thing I was relieved about was they weren't actual fires. Overall, the day was great. Once we were free from the closet, Tilly and I barely spoke. I had a feeling she was as confused as I was about our *almost* kiss. I knew she was coming around to liking me, but was she actually going to kiss me? My head is in shambles just thinking about it.

"Here, you have to wear this." Lina was going through my closet to help me pick an outfit for tonight.

"This?!" I gasp. It's a red lacy bodysuit with ruffled sleeves. It's basically see-through, except for the bra's padding. I've worn it out in the city on more than one occasion, but it feels a little scandalous for a small town.

"If you want to get Tilly's attention, this is the way to do it." She holds it up in front of me. My jaw drops open. I've never said anything about Tilly and me to her. "Oh please, you can deny it, but you two are so obvious. Just do us all a favor and get together already."

"I don't think she feels the same," I admit.

"Then you're as blind as she is. Of course, she feels the same. She's been so angry for months because she doesn't want to act on it. But I think she's finally coming around." Lina laughs.

"I assume you know we hooked up already?"

"Oh yeah, I think it's hysterical because she used to be the queen of one-night stands, and since you, she hasn't even been out," Lina says.

"Really?"

"You really don't see the way she looks at you?" Lina asks, raising an eyebrow.

"I don't," I admit.

"She cares for you. I don't know if she's ready to admit it, but she does. So wear this—maybe with some ripped jeans—and she won't be able to take her eyes off you," Lina says, giving me the bodysuit.

"Okay."

I grab a pair of jeans from my dresser as Lina sits on the bed to do her makeup. She is already dressed, wearing this cute off-the-shoulder black floral top and a mini skirt. Her legs are covered in tattoos—some quotes, some art.

"You ever think about getting one?" Lina asks, catching me staring at her legs.

"Oh no. I'm terrified of blood and needles. I'd pass out on the table." I shake my head.

"I love them. My ex was a tattoo artist in the city, so a lot of these I got for free," she says.

I head into the bathroom to change and let my curls free from the wrap I have them in. I like my natural hair; it looks much better than when I attempt to tame my mane. Lina says she is going to do my makeup, so I head back to the bedroom and sit next to her on the bed. She's quiet as she applies different things to my face, and I try to relax. I don't know why I am so nervous;

I've been out with Lina, Hattie, and Tilly before. But this time Tilly knows I am going. Part of me is praying she notices me and doesn't try going home with someone else like last time. Sure, that was months ago, but it still stings—right up until I see her look of terror.

"Okay, we're ready to go!" Lina announces, and I look in the mirror.

"Damn! You made me look good." I admire my curves and the fresh makeup. She knows what she's doing.

We grab our shoes on the way out, and Hattie is driving us all. She has to relieve the babysitter later, so she offers to be our designated driver. I wonder if she ever gets a night off from being a mom; most of the time she acts like our mom too, making sure we don't drink too much and we have water before going to bed. Tilly sits in the front with Hattie, so we slide in the back, not giving her a chance to see my outfit before we get there. But as we pull up to the bar, Tilly gets out and opens my door. I get out one foot at a time; with my luck and heels, I'll end up falling on my face. Tilly's jaw drops as she sees what I'm wearing. She struggles to pick up her jaw and take her eyes off my body. Oh, I am definitely going to have to thank Lina later.

"Beer?" Tilly asks when we go inside. Bill stops pouring a drink to gawk at me like a man. His jaw is on the floor, and I take great pleasure in that, especially considering how he usually ignores me.

"Yes, please." The rest of us find a table as Tilly orders.

"Holy shit, I didn't realize how good this would work! It's amazing," I whisper to Lina.

"Everyone has their eyes on you tonight. If you aren't going home with Tills, you're going home with someone," she winks.

Tilly brings over our drinks and takes the empty seat next to me. Our hands brush together as I reach for the frosty bottle. Wetness drips down the side of the bottle, her hands warmer than mine. We both pull away shyly; then I reach for the bottle again and press it to my lips. I can feel her gaze on me, but I'm not giving her the satisfaction of looking. Three beers and a round of shots later, Lina and Tilly are talking me into dancing.

"Come on! We can line dance!" they say, like I'm supposed to know what that is.

"I have no clue what that even is," I laugh.

"I'll teach you," Tilly says, holding out a hand and flashing me her perfect smile. She bats her blue eyes at me, and I cave.

"Fine." I toss back the rest of my drink, and everyone cheers.

Tilly's hand in mine feels right. It's just the perfect size despite our height and size difference. Her hand is warm while mine is still cold from holding the beer so tight. She leads me to the dance floor, which is basically the only spot in the bar that doesn't have any chairs or tables in it. The music is playing some song I've never heard, but my focus is on Tilly. She's wearing these long cargo shorts and a black tank top that's cropped to show her abs, with a button-up shirt over it. It's riding low, so I can even make out the tops of her tits.

"Come on, you just have to follow my lead," Tilly says and pulls me closer to her.

I glance at her feet, trying to figure out how to do this. She seems to be moving them in a square pattern, but that doesn't seem right. As soon as the song changes, she changes her footing completely, and I almost topple over trying to keep up. Tilly catches me by the waist, and my eyes lock onto hers. Instead of letting go, she pulls me in closer. Her body is hard like a rock wall against all my squishiness.

"I think I like this better," she murmurs quietly.

Her hands stay on my hips as we move slower against each other. It's a slow song that I'm convinced one of her friends put on for us. They are sneaky that way. So I wrap my arms around her neck, and I can feel the tiny goose bumps she has. She's staring at my breasts, and I'm waiting for the second she realizes I've caught her. But the song changes—probably because it's too slow for the bar—and she lets go of my waist. I start moving my hips, knowing this song I can dance to the beat of. I turn around to dance with Lina, but she's nowhere to be found. Instead, Tilly starts grinding behind me, and I gasp at the contact. Her hands are on the sides of my thighs, holding me as I grind my ass on her. I can feel her breath on my skin. Is it suddenly incredibly hot in here?

"Is this okay?" she whispers.

"Y-yes," I say, but I don't even know if she can hear me.

I don't stop moving; all I want is more friction, more of her body touching mine. I can feel the alcohol taking over. I'm pretty tipsy but not drunk—mostly in love with the way her body feels touching mine. It has been way too long since I've been touched by anyone but the showerhead, and I am desperate for more. I spin around and shake my body against hers. We're probably causing a scene, but I don't give a shit. All I care about right now is how amazing it feels to be touched by her.

"God, you are so beautiful," Tilly says, and before I have a chance to respond, she's pulling me in for a kiss.

Our lips smash together, her tongue slipping in my mouth, and I groan against her. For months now, we've been denying our chemistry and how we make each other feel. But in this moment Tilly doesn't seem to care. She tastes like beer and the limes she's been sucking on all night. Yet I don't pull away from her bitterness; she's somehow sweeter than I anticipate. Her tongue twirls around mine, and her hands grip my hips tightly. My hands tangle through her soft blonde hair, and she moans lightly into my mouth. Fuck. This is going to kill me if we keep teasing each other.

"Let's get out of here," Tilly says against my lips. I can feel her breathing as heavily as I am.

"O-okay," I mutter.

She takes me by the hand and leads me out the front door. I don't know if anyone even sees us, because my eyes are too focused on Tilly. I watch the back of her body as she pulls me through a sea of people and calls someone on her phone. I assume it's for a cab since we just left behind our ride and neither of us is in any shape to drive. When the one cab in town shows up two minutes later, my suspicions are confirmed. Tilly opens the cab door, and I slide in. Tilly walks around the other side and slips in next to me. She rattles off the orchard's address, and the car starts moving. Tilly pulls me closer to her, and her hand melts into mine.

Leaning in, she pushes my curls out of the way and whispers in my ear, "As soon as we're alone again I'm going to have my way with you."

I shiver in anticipation, only able to nod.

"I can see how bad you want this. Are you wet?" she whispers, and I can feel her breath on my ear.

"Yes," I whisper back, and she kisses my earlobe. I suck in a breath, and she tugs it between her teeth. Fuck. My hand grips her thigh, needing to touch any part of her right now.

"I love seeing how desperate you are for this," she says.

She is going to pay for teasing me later. I can't say or do anything right now, but the second we are in a bedroom, I'll be the one in control. Her lips stay on my neck as I keep my composure, willing myself not to moan aloud for the cabdriver.

SIXTEEN

Tilly

I pull Bells inside my house; the second the door shuts behind us, we're like magnets pulling toward each other. We kick off our shoes, and her hands find my hips. I lead her to my bedroom and flick the light on. This time I am going to take my time with her body. I don't know when I'll have an opportunity like this again, and I'm not going to waste it. This isn't the time to define what this is, so I'm going to enjoy the moment.

"Are you sure this is okay?" she pulls back from kissing me to ask.

I take her hand, leading it into my panties, and she gasps. "Does this show you how okay with it I am?"

"Y-yes," she mutters, and a blush runs through her cheeks. She pulls her hand back, and I smirk at her.

"What's the matter, baby? Didn't realize how wet I was?"

"I want you to undress me this time," she commands firmly. I nod; I'm not going to argue with her. When a beautiful woman tells you to get her naked, you say yes. Or better yet, you say nothing and strip her as fast as humanly possible.

I unbutton the front of her jeans and let them fall to the ground. Her shirt, which looks more like lingerie, is tucked into them. She stands before me in this red lacy bodysuit with her breasts popping out the top, and I groan. She smiles proudly, knowing how much this is killing me. As I go to touch one of her breasts, she moves away.

"Did I say you could touch me?" she crosses her arms.

"I guess not. Should I get undressed?"

"No. I want you on the bed," she commands, and I nod.

I sit on the bed. Bells climbs in next to me and pulls me in for a kiss. She's got her hands on my chest, digging them through my hair. When I go to touch her, she hits my hand away—not in a mean way or in a way that even hurts, more of a gentle shooing away.

"I told you not to touch me yet. This is payback for your little stunt in the cab." She narrows her dark eyes at me.

"Fine," I grumble, and she leans back into the bed, unbuttoning my jeans.

Her face moves next to mine as I fall back into the pillows. She slips her hands into my jeans and panties, and I moan, loudly. "Oh, fucking hell."

"God, you're so wet and needy for me." Bells' eyes twinkle with delight. I've never seen her like this, but it's hot as fuck. She's taking control, and I want to do anything she says.

I'm going to reply—something snarky—when she brushes her fingers across my clit, and I moan again. She's whispering dirty things in my ear, and I'm gasping for more. Her fingers slide through my wetness, and I groan. God, it's embarrassing how wet I am for her.

"I've been thinking about you. How bad I wanted to touch you again," she admits in my ear. This time, she's the one to nibble gently on my earlobe. I buck my hips against her hand, begging silently for more friction.

"I don't think so. I'm going to make you work for it," she says, pushing my hips back down into the bed.

"Fuck," I gasp as she pulls her fingers out of my panties.

"I need to hear you beg for it."

"I want it—God, I fucking want it."

"That doesn't sound like begging. I guess we could just stop." Bells smirks and moves away, but I pull her face into mine.

"I want you. God, I want you to fuck me. Please."

"A little better." She smiles and slides her hand down my panties again.

Two fingers swirl around my clit before sliding inside me. I gasp, soft moans and pants escaping my lips as she pumps them in and out.

"Now, tell me how bad you want this," she whispers in my ear.

"I—I fucking want this. I want you," I say breathlessly.

"Better." She pumps her fingers harder, and I moan.

"Oh, Bells! Yes!" Her thumb touches my clit, and I can feel her hand getting soaked from me.

"God, just fucking touch me. Do you know how long I've been waiting for you to fuck me again?" I admit. I don't care—if she wants me to beg for her, I'll be on my knees if that's what it takes.

"Good. Now get down on your knees like a good girl and work for it." Bells moves her hand out of my panties and sucks her fingers clean. The action alone could make me cum, but I'm too shocked by her words for my body to do anything.

"You want me on my knees?" I mutter.

"Yes, now. Show me how bad you want to be fucked," Bells commands and spreads her deliciously thick thighs. Holy hell, where was this woman dropped from?

I flick the buttons of her bodysuit open, and it flies apart, giving me a perfect view of her pussy. She has a landing strip leading to her clit, and I groan, seeing her juices coat the lips of her pussy. Leaning down, I kiss it gently. Bells gasps, and I lick through her folds. Her sweet taste coats my tongue before I take her clit in my mouth. I suck lightly, and Bells moans, her thighs closing around my ears. She might be accidentally suffocating me with her thighs, and I don't care. Because right now I'm making this woman moan like there's no neighbor in sight. She's louder than she was that first night and definitely wetter. I know she says she doesn't usually come with anyone, but I'm feeling much more confident. I tweak her nipple with my free hand, and she says my name. Well, it is more of a slow moan.

"Fuck, fuck, fuck." She curses as I switch hands so I can slide a finger inside her tight pussy while I suck on her clit. I hum against her, and her legs shake.

"Yes! Oh my God! Stop!" she yells, and I pull away immediately, looking up at her with worried eyes.

"Everything okay?"

"Yes! Just so freaking sensitive. I think that's the closest I've gotten to coming with someone," she admits.

"Do you want me to keep going?" I'm eager to please, or whatever she wants from me.

"No, I want you to get your reward." She smirks and twirls her fingers at me.

I wipe my face on the back of my arm and shrug off my button-down shirt. I'm still wearing my shorts and a crop top, with my nipples pebbling through.

"Take everything off," she commands, and I jump up.

In record time, everything is off and on the floor. I climb back into the bed as Bells removes her bodysuit. She's completely naked, and I'm in absolute awe. How the hell can anyone look at her and not be? She has all these gorgeous curves and rolls that add to her breasts that I want to lay my head on. I imagine they could be the best pillows.

"Come here," she whispers, and I lay next to her.

It starts off slower this time—her kissing me and our bodies colliding. Everything feels so different with no clothes on. There's no fabric between us, and she slips her hand to my pussy. Her fingers slide inside me, and my head falls back. If it could, I'm sure it would fall off with how good her fingers feel. They're bigger and thicker than mine, so it feels much different than when I usually take care of things. She curls them inside me, and I let out an embarrassingly loud moan.

"That's what I want to hear. Don't hold back for me," Bells praises. I'm never one to have a praise kink, but God, just seeing how happy my moans make her makes me want to make more.

I whimper in pleasure as she rubs her thumb over my wet clit. I fall into her this time, her hand somewhere in between us and my body melting into hers. We're both starting to sweat; the summer is here, and I didn't think to turn on the AC when we came in. Her body is hot, like the temperature could fry an egg. But she looks blissful as she teases me. Her fingers are moving achingly slow now that she knows I'm close, and I know what she wants. She must have a thing for begging, because I've never had a woman tease me like this before.

"Please be nice," I say quietly, looking into her dark eyes.

"I don't know; it seems like you could live without it." She shrugs, and I stop her hand from leaving me.

"Keep your hand inside me and fuck me before I get my vibrator and do it myself," I command.

"Hmm, that sounds nice. Maybe we should do that instead, since I don't hear any begging?" She smirks, and I know how much she's enjoying this.

"Bells, I'm begging you. Please don't stop. Please."

It clearly works, because as I let go of her hand, she starts to finger-fuck me again. Her thumb rubs circles around my clit, and I can feel my orgasm building. Holy hell, this woman might be the literal death of me.

"Yes! Yes! Right there!" I scream out as the orgasm starts crashing over me like waves. I can't see or feel anything but pleasure as I fall back into the pillows. Bells doesn't stop until I'm batting her hand away and she's licking them clean. I peek open one eye to see that.

"Wow, I can't believe we just did that," she mutters so quietly I'm not sure if I'm supposed to say anything.

"Any regrets?" I ask.

"Shit, I didn't know you heard that." She blushes. "No regrets. I'm just surprised, is all," she admits.

"Like you didn't plan it, wearing that outfit tonight." I raise an eyebrow at her.

"In my defense, Lina picked it out for me." She laughs.

"She knows what I like." I shrug.

"So, I should—" She goes to stand, but I catch her arm.

"Spend the night. If you want," I add quickly.

"Okay." She nods with a smile, and I relax a bit.

We've gone about this all backward. One-night stands before we even knew the other's names, but maybe this is the chance to fix things. We can't rewrite history, but maybe we can start over? Bells slips back into the bed beside me, and I extend my arm for her to cuddle into. She hesitantly lays her head on my chest, and we're both quiet. We should probably be talking about whatever the hell this is, but instead she closes her eyes, and I listen to her breathing as she falls asleep. Somewhere in my overthinking, I end up closing my eyes too. I feel her body heat, the soft, quiet snores, and the rising of her chest. I don't remember the last time I fall asleep next to someone who wasn't Hattie or Lina. I don't do sleepovers, especially with one-night stands. But the longer I lie next to Bells, the easier it feels to fall asleep.

Which only scares the living shit out of me. If she isn't a one-night stand anymore, then what is she? I know I have feelings for her, but I don't think it will ever be anything. Considering the way we've fought the last few months, having her in my bed like this is the last thing on my mind. But now I'm not so sure I want to let her go.

SEVENTEEN

Bells

I wake up with a start as I feel someone move beside me. Considering I usually sleep alone, I'm petrified about what creature has crawled into bed with me. But when I open my eyes to see Tilly and an unfamiliar room, my head starts pounding. I don't remember how we got here, and I definitely don't remember falling asleep in her bed. I'm naked under the sheets, so we clearly had sex. As I think about it, I get glimpses of her touching and tasting me, her body begging me to fuck her, and us falling asleep together. I almost went home last night, but she asked me to stay for whatever reason. She probably felt bad with how late it was.

But now it's morning, and I have a million things to do at home. So I slip out of the bed and grab my scattered clothes from the floor. It's going to be a pain in the ass to get dressed in the clothes from last night just to walk home twenty-five feet. But it isn't like I can slip next door naked. I grab my socks and start down the stairs quietly. I'm tiptoeing on each step, but as I reach the last step, I see a figure in the doorway, and I almost scream.

"Bells?" Hattie's voice keeps me from screaming, and I step down the last step.

"Hattie?" I raise an eyebrow. What is she doing here so early?

"Bells!" Ollie peeks out from behind Hattie, and I smile.

"Hey, Ollie." I smile. Hattie and I exchange an awkward glance. It's obvious I'm attempting to flee a one-night stand.

"Is Aunt Tilly awake?" Ollie asks excitedly.

"Uh." I freeze, unsure of how to answer that.

"Why don't we start breakfast, and I'll check on Tilly?" Hattie says, ushering her son in the opposite direction.

When he's out of earshot, I grab my shoes and start to put them on. Hattie returns and looks at me curiously.

"Tilly's upstairs, but she's not exactly… decent," I say delicately. I feel like I've been caught by my parents sneaking someone over.

"We usually do Saturday morning breakfast here. I should've realized from last night she might not be, uh, up to it," Hattie says softly.

"No worries, I'm just headed out," I say awkwardly.

"Do you want to stay?"

"Oh, no thank you. I have a lot to do today. But I'll catch you guys later." I smile. Pushing the front door open, I almost slam into Lina holding a tray of freshly baked cinnamon rolls.

"Oh! Hello! Looks like someone had a good night," Lina says smugly.

I blush. It isn't like I can deny it. I silently pray I'm not going to run into anyone else in my very short walk home. I mean, how many people need to know what Tilly and I did last night?

"I told you that top would work." Lina winks.

"Okay! See you all later!" I race out the front door and toward my house, not stopping for a second until I'm safely inside.

I toss my clothes right into the laundry and head for the shower. I need to clear my head and wash last night off my skin. Not that I regret it. If anything, I'll be thinking of it for days to come. I can feel the way Tilly kissed my skin, the way her tongue felt on my body, and how we just melted into each other. Everything will be reminding me of her until I push it out of my mind.

We've done this once before, and this will be no different. I know I have feelings for her, but I'm not about to go all Ted Mosby and think there's something more here. She and I want a hookup, to let go of all that tension we have. But that's all it is—it's just weird she asked me to stay last night. The hot water washes over my body, and I relax. Pouring shampoo in my hands, I run my fingers through my hair and close my eyes. If I don't think about it too hard, I can imagine it's Tilly touching me. There was something different about last night. Maybe just because we know each other better than we did months ago.

I rinse my body off, wrap one of my fluffy towels around myself, and head for my room. Laying down on my bed, I reach to my nightstand for my phone. It isn't there, and I realize I didn't come in here before I showered. Did I leave it in my clothes? The jeans I was wearing have pockets, but I don't remember seeing anything in them. Does that mean… Oh, shit. I left my phone at Tilly's house somewhere. It isn't bad enough that I left like a bad one-night stand and ran into her two best friends on the way out. Now I have to redo my walk of shame to get my phone? Nope—you know what? She can keep it. I'll buy a new one. Okay, that seems bad for the environment, but I definitely am not going over there right now to get it.

I don't even have a way to ask her for it without going over there. And it's not like I remember where I left it. Maybe I left it at the bar—that would be better. Not that I want to go all the way there to see if they maybe have my phone, either, though. Ugh. I'm usually more responsible than this. Now I've made a mess of everything in one night. That's what I get for getting drunk and hooking up with my irresistibly hot employee. She isn't just my employee, but I don't know what else she is. Is there a word for someone who hates you but also fucks you and is your employee but also sort of a friend?

I decide to get dressed and FaceTime El—she'll know what to do. I can't lie here overthinking. So I throw on some workout clothes and open my laptop. Unfortunately, she doesn't pick up, and I grumble. She texts me a few minutes later, telling me she's traveling but can text me. I'm about to email and explain I left my phone at Tilly's house when I remember I can send texts from my laptop. I log in with the cloud and start messaging her.

ME: I hooked up with Tilly again, last night. And left my phone there 😳

EL: How was the sex?? Better this time or last time??

ME: So much better. I almost came with her eating me out which you know NEVER happens.

EL: holy shit! She was that good?? I need details or the number of her friend

ME: We went to a bar with friends of ours, got drunk and handsy in a cab. Then went back to her place. It was hot as hell and then she asked me to stay over

EL: So why are you texting me and not still at her house?? It's like nine in the morning!

ME: I sort of did the walk of shame…

ME: and her two best friends caught me leaving…

EL: omg

ME: Now I feel like an idiot bc I left my phone and I see her all the time

EL: maybe she feels the same? Like that it was just a hookup?

ME: but what if I don't want it to be just a hookup?

EL: maybe she feels the same

ME: but how would I know??

EL: uh maybe by talking to her??

ME: gross. no.

EL: LMAO.

EL: valid

Groaning, I push my laptop aside and decide to distract myself. I eye the pumpkin muffin that Lina brought over. It has pot in it, and right now I need to relax. I take a few bites, and I don't feel anything, so I take a few more. Lina said not to have more than half the muffin, but it tastes so good. I listen to her despite wanting more and wrap the other half up.

Heading downstairs, I start catching up on the chores around the house. The laundry is first, where I double-check for my phone, and then the dishes. I start to feel the weed kicking in, and my brain is light and airy—almost as if every thought is like cotton candy instead of sharp potato chips. I don't know if that makes sense, but it makes sense to me. I decide to put on Twilight while I clean; it's a comfort movie, even if I hate being referred to as the main character.

I'm sweeping up when I decide to take a break and lie on the couch. The blankets look too cozy not to relax under, and I can take a few-minute break. Five minutes later, I'm itching for a snack. I don't have a lot of choices in my fridge, but I settle on a bag of croutons with ranch dressing to dip them in and some gummy bears. I sit back on the couch and watch Bella and Edward fall in love. Will I ever have that? Do I even want that?

Maybe not some toxic love between a vampire and a human, but real, life-changing love. When Taylor and I broke up, I didn't really bat an eye. It was more annoying knowing I'd be working with them all the time. They're competitive and only wanted the job I did, so I couldn't have it. But maybe I wasn't really in love with her. We got along fine, and we dated for a while, but I never felt that life-altering spark—not the way I feel about Tilly. Not that I'm in love with her either; what she and I have is mostly sexual tension.

I crush a bag of pepperoni slices and a chocolate bar before the munchies start to fade. Lina must grow some potent shit. I've never had a high like this before. I feel relaxed, carefree, and just want to nap—now that the munchies are gone. As the end credits of the movie roll, I change the laundry I forgot about into the dryer before I turn on New Moon. It's sort of depressing, but you can't binge the saga without watching all the movies— which is apparently what I'm going to do now.

As I close my eyes, I hear the music playing in the background and the vampires talking—Bella begging to be turned into one and Edward saying no. I wonder how I'd handle being a vampire. It seems like there's a lot of running involved, which I wouldn't like. But you don't sweat, and I'd be fast, so maybe it wouldn't be so bad? I don't think I could handle the whole blood-drinking part of it, though. I'd have to find a way around that or something. Do vampires faint? If they do, is it ever over blood? With my luck I'd be the first vampire fainting when they try to feed.

Tilly pops into my head, and I think she'd make a good vampire. She's already pale and beautiful, but she's strong and doesn't have a problem with blood. Maybe I'd be better off as a wolf, but it seems like a lot of work not to shift and lose your clothes. It's not like I could run around topless like the male wolves. I mean, I probably could, but I'd also get arrested for it. Maybe Tilly knows a trick for getting me over my blood phobia. I reach for my phone and realize it's still at her house. Maybe I should go over there and get it. But as I stand, I see Edward shirtless on-screen, and all I can think about are those memes where he's telling her, "This is the skin of a killer," and I burst out laughing.

EIGHTEEN

Tilly

"Tills!" Hattie calls through the bedroom door.

I groan before answering. "What?"

"It's breakfast time! Get dressed and come downstairs."

"Fine! Give me five!" I call back.

I hear her walk down the stairs, and I turn over—groaning. My head is killing me. How much did I have to drink last night? Usually, I set up a glass of water and some Tylenol on my nightstand, but I guess drunk me wasn't very helpful this time. Suddenly, I sit up, remembering Bells in my bed last night. She spent the night, didn't she? But where is she? I glance toward the bathroom, but she isn't in there either. I guess she went home. Did she sneak out before Hattie and Lina came over? I guess there is only way one way to find out.

I get out of bed, toss on some pajamas, and head to the bathroom to tame my messy hair. It's a mix between sex hair and bedhead—something I don't want to explain to my friends, let alone Ollie. Once that's tamed, I brush my teeth. As I'm about to leave my bedroom, I hear an unfamiliar chime go off. It happens twice more, and I follow the sound to a cell phone on the floor under my bed. I pick it up and recognize it as Bells's phone. She carries the damn thing around wherever she goes. I'm shocked she left it here. But maybe that shows how much of a rush she was in when she was trying to leave.

I had thought we might talk in the morning. About whatever was going on between us. But now she's gone, and I guess that's my answer. I could be a one-night stand; I've done it plenty of times with other women. I just never usually had to see those women again on a daily basis. I slip the phone in my pocket and head downstairs before Hattie comes looking for me again.

"Look who's finally up," Lina teases as she sips her coffee out of one of my mugs.

"It's barely nine a.m.," I groan. I need coffee and some Tylenol before I get into this with them.

"Someone was up late," Hattie muses, and I can't tell if she's just commenting or she's jealous.

"Where's Ollie?" I look around.

"He's watching TV. There's a shark documentary on that he was begging me to see," Hattie explains.

"Plus, it gives us grownups a chance to chat about the redhead making a run for it this morning." Lina smirks.

Shit, so they *did* see Bells leaving. I decide to play it off. "I'm not sure what you're talking about."

Hattie and Lina both roll their eyes at me as I sit at the kitchen table. I grab a cinnamon roll off the plate and take a hearty bite. Fuck, Lina is such a good baker. The pastry melts in my mouth and goes perfectly with a fresh cup of coffee.

"Bells was in a mad dash out of here this morning, are we to believe she snuck in without your knowledge?" Lina asks.

"We hooked up last night." I sigh. There was no use hiding it from them.

"We know that, but why was she running out?" Lina asks.

"I don't know. I was sleeping." I shrug.

"Maybe she heard Ollie and I coming in?" Hattie offers quietly. I hope this conversation wasn't making her uncomfortable.

"She left behind her phone," I say, pulling it out of my pocket and putting it on the table.

"Oh my god, like a modern-day Cinderella." Lina laughs. "Have you looked through it?"

"No!" I gasp.

"Why not? Maybe she wants you to?" Lina says.

"It's not her business what's on her phone," Hattie adds.

"Fine, I'm just saying. Maybe you'd have more information if you saw her recent texts." Lina shrugs.

"I'm not reading her texts," I say. But just as I do, the phone chimes and lights up with a new text.

"Wait, this person is talking about you!" Lina grabs the phone and reads the latest message aloud. "How was the sex?? Better this time or last time??"

"Oh my God," Hattie mumbles.

"Who's she texting?" I ask, my mouth getting suddenly dry.

"Uh, it just says *Bestie*. So her version of Hattie and me," Lina says. "We can't read what she's saying without unlocking the phone, but she must be texting from an iPad or her computer. These are coming in right now."

The phone chimes again.

"It says, 'Holy shit! She was that good?? I need details or the number of her friend,'" Lina reads aloud. I blush, and Hattie spills the coffee she's pouring into her mug.

"Maybe let's not read these." I reach for the phone, and Lina nods.

She's the only one I told about Hattie's crush on me. I want to be sensitive, but I also don't want to treat her with kid gloves. I'm constantly overthinking everything when it comes to our friendship. But it's obvious she's uncomfortable hearing about me and Bells being intimate.

"So, are you two seeing each other now?" Hattie asks, clearing her throat.

"We didn't really talk about it. I thought we'd talk today, but she left before we could," I admit.

"Maybe that's the answer?" Hattie says.

"What do you mean?" I raise an eyebrow at her.

"Well, I've never really had a one-night stand. But don't you typically stick around if you want to see the person again?" Hattie sips her coffee. She isn't saying this maliciously, but it does hurt a bit to hear.

"I mean, yeah, but there are a lot of reasons she could have left," I say.

"Yeah, maybe she had work to do," Lina points out.

"Without her phone?" Hattie says.

"That's why we should read it and see what she's thinking." Lina eyes the phone that's chiming in my hands.

"No." I shake my head. "If I'm going to find out what she's thinking, it's going to be in person. Not because I snooped in her phone. But maybe Hattie's right..."

Is Hattie right? Bells made it obvious what she wants by leaving. I shouldn't be second-guessing her motives when she couldn't get out of here fast enough this morning. Which is fine. It's not like I suddenly want to fall in love or some shit. It would be easier if I didn't sleep with my boss, but I've done worse things.

"Can you bring her back her phone on the way home?" I ask Lina.

"Are you sure?" She looks at me skeptically.

"Yes. I have to check the animals, and I don't have time," I lie as I slide her the phone.

"Okay." Lina nods.

I head upstairs to change into work clothes. They can keep hanging out, but I need to feed the horses and use my muscles for something productive. I feel too anxious to sit around talking about this. I wave goodbye to my friends on the way out and unlock the barn. It wouldn't be the first time my friends hung out at my house when I wasn't home. We all have an open-door policy when it comes to our homes.

I let the horses free, give them their breakfast, and then take a walk toward the apple fields. I haven't checked in on the apples in a few days, and it can't hurt to look. We open in twenty minutes, so there are already people hard at work everywhere else on the orchard. It's technically my day off, but I can't help myself.

I take the hike to the orchard and walk the fields. There are new baskets at the end of each aisle, and the trees look amazing. Thankfully no wildlife has gotten to them yet, so most of the apples are still hanging beautifully on the branches. The bright green trees, different-colored apples, and the smell of freshly cut grass make me close my eyes for a moment and take it all in. Maybe this is what I need. There's a light breeze, and I take a deep breath as I walk down the empty paths.

We keep the paths down between the aisles of apple trees freshly mowed so people can walk through without a problem. Some families have strollers or walking aids, and although the grass is even, it's easier to walk through when it's cut closely. We try to make it accessible to everyone. That's something Benny pushed for—especially at the end, when she was too sick to walk along the paths herself. At least once a week, I'd push her in the wheelchair up here, and we'd walk through the lanes to make sure the apples were growing okay. We'd talk about the next season even though both of us knew she wasn't going to make it for the next one.

I clench my fists at the memory. I knew she was sick, but it didn't make losing her any easier. I've come to somewhat understand her choice to give Bells the orchard. She's doing an amazing job and has really turned the place around. Everything is bustling, and I know we're sold out of tickets for the next few weekends—something that hasn't happened in years. Maybe she wanted to keep it in the family, or maybe she had an idea that Bells would take over the place like this. I'm still worried she's fixing it up to sell, but for the time being, it seems unlikely.

The only thing that bothers me is feeling like she thought I couldn't handle the orchard on my own. Did something happen where she thought I was no longer able to handle it? She always promised it to me, and then all of a sudden, it was out of my hands. I wish she could see how much I'm taking on and how much I handled everything at the end when she was sick. She never wanted to talk about it, but I thought that was just because she was scared. I always thought she saw me as family, the way I saw her as the mother I needed—but maybe that was more embellished than I thought. In the end, I guess it comes down to her wanting to leave it to a blood relative, and I was just a teenage runaway she took in.

I hear people coming toward the aisle I'm in, and I know I need to get the tractor back. Someone forgot to bring it back down yesterday and while I didn't mind the walk up to the apple trees, something tells me the staff will. The staff will need it for the hayrides and transportation of the day. I wipe my eyes, suck in a sharp breath, and take one last look at the orchard. Everything is picture-perfect for today, and I have no doubt with the growing crowds Bells promised, we'll be set.

Hopping back on the tractor, I watch as couples, families, old people, and everyone in between head toward the apple trees. Everyone is smiling, the kids running up to the trees and parents telling them to be careful. I'm glad Bells' influencer day has brought in all kinds of crowds. I didn't think that was possible, but I'm proven wrong about her again—not that I'm ready to admit it to her yet.

Bells' smile pops in my head as I head back, and I can't help but smile myself. I've been an idiot lately when it comes to her, and as much as I want to blame the alcohol or the overwhelming sexual tension, I know it's more than that. She's getting under my skin, and I don't think I mind it. Something about her makes everything different. Every time I think she's going to change things for the worse, things end up better and stronger than before. Maybe that's what she's doing to me too.

NINETEEN

Bells

"**W**here are you headed?" Tilly asks, standing by the tractor. Her arms are exposed, glistening in the sun with a few beads of sweat.

"Oh, I was going to pick some apples. I haven't actually done that yet," I admit.

"You haven't picked apples this season, or ever?"

"Well, if you count the summer I stayed here, I did. But since then, not so much," I say shyly.

"Get up here, we're going now." Tilly commands and climbs up on the tractor. It's not attached to the trailer, but there's enough room for me to sit too. She takes my hand and helps me climb up. Thankfully, I thought to wear my boots today.

"What's your favorite kind of apple?" she asks. It's one of the first times I've talked to her since our night together. We see each other every day, but it's not like we have a lot of chances to talk about anything with people around. Plus, I kind of get the feeling she doesn't want to talk when she had Lina return my phone to me. Like that wasn't awkward as fuck.

"I don't know." I furrow my brows together. Even though I know the names of all the apples now, I don't know if I could tell the difference between most.

"Then we'll start at the beginning and do a taste test," she decides.

"You're coming along?" I ask, surprised.

"Yeah, if you'll have me." She smiles.

"Of course." My stomach turns to butterflies as I think about spending the day with her.

"Okay, we'll start here and make our way down," she decides.

"Do you have a favorite apple?" I ask.

"Of course I do. I'm partial to Pink Lady apples." She winks.

"What do those taste like?"

"I'll let you be the judge of that." She reaches into the tree and pulls down a perfectly round apple. She rubs it on the edge of her shirt and hands it to me.

"Shouldn't we clean it first?" I wrinkle my nose.

Tilly tilts her head to look at me. "You're kidding, right? I picked it fresh from the tree. I'll take a bite first if you need convincing."

I nod, so she laughs and takes a bite out of one side of the pink apple.

"Satisfied?" The juice from the apple runs down her chin, and it gives me a flashback to the last time I was dripping down her chin.

"Mmm." I mumble and take the apple from her. She wipes her arm on her mouth, and I take a small bite of the apple. It's extra sweet and juicy—it's really good.

"So?" she prompts.

"I like it a lot. It's really sweet." I smile.

"Pink Lady apples are always the first to blossom and last to be harvested, each one soaks up about 200 days of sunshine," she explains.

"Wow. Do you know a lot of random apple facts?"

"A hazard of the job." She shrugs. "John Cripps is the plant breeder who naturally cross-bred the first-ever Cripps Pink apple in Australia in 1973. The best of these apples were then branded Pink Lady."

"I should have you send me some of these facts for the Instagram. Maybe we can do a weekly 'Did you know?' about apples?" I suggest.

"That would be cool. I used to suggest to Benny that during the week we could have a guided tour of the orchard, but she didn't think anyone would come to that." She sighs.

"Wait, that's a great idea. We could do it on Wednesdays, since that's our slow day. It can be run by you, and eventually you can train one or two others to do the same. Everyone gets a taste of each apple on the tour and all the facts in your brain," I say excitedly.

"Really?" She looks at me, surprised.

"Yeah, it's a great idea." I smile. "We'll have to get together to talk specifics, but it definitely sounds great." I nod.

"Awesome." Tilly smiles. "Don't eat the whole thing. Toss the apple by the stump and follow me."

I follow her direction. It feels weird throwing away a perfectly good apple, but she's right—I can't eat entire apples of each one we try. So I follow her to the next row, and she hands me a dark red apple. This time she doesn't take a bite first, and I look at her warily.

"It's still safe, but I don't like Red Delicious apples. To me, they're bitter."

I take a bite, and sure enough, my mouth puckers right up. I spit out the small bite and toss the apple to the side. Frowning, I look at Tilly as she starts laughing.

"That was disgusting!" I wish I had water or something to clean out my mouth.

"I know. They're popular because they're one of the oldest apples, but that was mainly because they're the most durable to transport—not because they're the most delicious. We always get people asking for them, but I don't get it." Tilly laughs.

"Well, I never want one of those again." I frown.

"Good to know. Let's head to the next row—I think you'll like them."

"Which ones are these?" I ask, looking at the reddish apples with a hint of yellow streaks.

"These are Fuji apples. They're very sweet, often compared to apple juice, so I think you may enjoy them." She smiles and takes a bite before handing me one.

I take a bite, and it's much better than the Red Delicious—but that's not really saying anything. It does remind me of apple juice, and it's a little crunchier than the Pink Lady apple.

"The Fuji apple was created in Fujisaki, Aomori, Japan. They crossed Red Delicious apples and Ralls Janet apples to create it back in the 1960s," Tilly says.

"I like this one, but Pink Lady is still my favorite so far," I say.

"Got it." She nods, moving us along to the next aisle.

We try four more kinds of apples, including Golden Delicious, Granny Smith, and Gala. By the end, I'm sure that Pink Lady is my favorite, but I'm definitely appled-out. I feel like I've eaten fifty apples when, in reality, I probably didn't even have one full one. All the different tastes and tartness are an interesting change.

"So how do you feel now that you've officially gone apple picking?" Tilly asks.

"Good. I feel like I know a lot more about apples, at least—which is probably good information to have." I laugh.

"Are you doing anything the rest of the day?" she asks, and my heart skips a beat. Is she going to ask me out?

"Uh, no?"

"You should come over, and I can teach you how to make apple pie. Lina, Hattie, and I are making them for the pie-eating contest next week."

My heart sinks, realizing it's a friendly invite. I mean, of course it is—I'm her boss. She doesn't want to cross that line again and is trying to make things less awkward between us.

"Oh, sure. Should I bring anything?"

"Nah, just clothes you don't mind baking in. It can get a little messy, and I don't have any aprons," Tilly says.

"I think I have some. I'll swing by my house before I stop by later. What time are you starting?"

"Around six." Tilly checks her watch. "I can text you if the time changes."

"Perfect." I smile.

It's quiet as she gives me a ride back to the main side of the orchard on the tractor. All you can hear is the motor, and we don't make small talk. I don't know if she's nervous or just ran out of things to say. I'm too busy overthinking. The way she smells like apples and fresh-cut grass is intoxicating. I've never been someone who wanted to be with someone so nature-y or outdoorsy, but fuck—just smelling her, I can't imagine anything else. There's something hot about a woman who works with her hands and takes care of business. I mean, like literally. Of course, my body is a little confused, and a shiver runs down my spine thinking of the last time she took care of my business.

"You okay?" Tilly asks as she helps me off the tractor.

"Of course," I say quickly.

"Okay—you just look a little flushed, is all." She tilts her head.

"Must be the heat! These boots are quite hot," I lie.

"Definitely a change from those heels of yours." She winks. Before I have a chance to respond, I'm sneaking toward my house to get ready for later.

TWENTY

Bells

"Is there a wrong way to mix?" I ask as Tilly pours ingredients into the bowl.

"Just stir in every direction until there aren't any lumps," she says.

I can cook a few things, but I've never been a baker. So I take the wooden spoon and mix around as much as I can. She's still adding things, so I pause each time she does.

"Do you want to cut up the apples or help me make the filling?" she asks as we wait for the latest batch of dough to proof.

"Uh, I can do either with some instructions."

"Take a seat, take this peeler, and start peeling apples. There's no wrong way, but we don't want any skin. It doesn't taste as good when it's cooked," she instructs.

"Do you guys do the pie-eating contest every year?" I ask.

"Yes, it was Benny's idea. She'd been doing it for at least five years before I got here," Tilly says.

"Wow, so it's a tradition of sorts."

"Yeah. I think she started it because it was something your family does every year."

"What?" I stop peeling to look at Tilly.

"What? That's what she told me." Tilly looks at me cautiously.

"That's really weird," I mumble.

"Who's that?"

"My family is like the CEOs of being fancy. I can't imagine them ever wanting to compete in a pie-eating contest. The mess alone would stress them enough to get more Botox." I shake my head, trying to imagine my mother doing one.

"I believe she said when everyone is a kid, it's a family tradition. But everyone grows up and then it stops. So she brought it here to relive a little of that magic," Tilly explains.

I smile. It's nice hearing about my aunt but also learning a little bit of the family lore that I'd otherwise never know about. It's not like my parents ever went around talking about their childhoods. As far as they're concerned, anything in the past doesn't count—unless it can make them money. Which is probably why they keep me around. My mother has been hounding me for months now. Why haven't I sold yet? Why haven't I signed over the place to them? What's the big hold-up, and why am I spending so much time up here? I haven't seen them since the funeral, but even though I suggested she come see the place, she still said no. To her, this place is something to inherit, and if she can't squeeze any money out of it, then she isn't interested.

I'm a little worried that things might change if she gets wind of how well we're doing. We're making a profit again, and it has only taken a few weeks. I don't want her to show up and try to take the place to the bank now that I've turned things around. So for the time being I keep telling her I'm working on things and, when I can, I'll be selling the place. It's a lie. I know I have no intention of selling, but it's easier than trying to explain it to my family. They'd probably ostracize me the way they did my aunt. If you don't run in the same circles they do, they don't talk to you.

I refocus on peeling the apples, making sure I don't accidentally peel the skin off my fingers. I'm not sure that's something

I can do, but I don't want to find out. Each peeled apple goes into a bowl, which Tilly takes and slices into small cubes. She says the smaller the pieces, the easier the apples bake in the pie. Nothing is worse than biting into a pie and it still being raw.

"Do you make the top look different?" I ask.

"What do you mean? Like the pie lattice?" she asks, confused.

Of course, she knows that's what it's called. "Yes."

"We could. I usually do the standard apple-pie lace. What do you have in mind?"

"I'm not sure, but maybe we could make them all different? It might add to the marketability of the event," I suggest.

"I think I have cookie cutters here somewhere." She pauses to look around the kitchen and comes across a bucket of shapes. She looks through them and pulls out ones that are different-sized apples, hearts, and leaves.

"Very festive," I nod.

"Is there a certain way to do it? I don't think I've ever used a cookie cutter," I say sheepishly.

"Even to make cookies?" She chuckles.

"Uh, only if you count the ones that come precut that you place on a tray," I admit.

"Come here." She waves me over.

Wrapping her arms around my body, she puts her hands on top of mine. She grabs the dough from the fridge she's cooling and puts the dough I just mixed in the fridge to settle. She has me push the dough with a roller, then with my hands, until it's perfectly flat. Then she places the cookie cutters along the dough as close as possible, cutting out a variety of shapes.

"We still have to make the inside of the apple pies, but that doesn't take too long, and it would be good to let these chill a bit in the fridge," Tilly says.

"Okay." I nod. She gets a tray, covers it with parchment paper, and then dusts some flour over it.

"If you dust your hands in the flour, it helps keep the dough from sticking to you," she explains.

"Got it." I stick my hands in the bag and coat them, but Tilly starts laughing. "What?"

"I sort of mean just a little." She laughs.

"Well, it's too late now." I shrug and start moving the dough shapes to the tray.

When I'm done, my hands are still covered in flour, so I poke Tilly's nose gently, leaving some behind. She laughs and pokes me in the cheek with her flour-covered hand. I take a little more on my hand and go to poke her face again, but when she moves at the last second, I end up covering her cheek completely. My jaw drops, but Tilly doesn't miss a beat and grabs a handful to dump on my head. We're hysterical, laughing at this point, just wasting the flour. As we toss it at each other, some falls to the floor, and as I move to get her, I end up falling on my ass.

"Oh, shit!" She stumbles toward me with a hand extended to help me, but I'm all laughs when I use her hand to pull her to the floor with me. Except she ends up falling right over me, and her body collapses on mine.

Her body is on top of me, and I gasp at the close contact. All I can smell is fresh-cut grass and apples. I don't know if that's her natural scent or some kind of body wash, but either way I want to keep smelling it.

"I want you," she growls in my ear.

"What about the pies?"

"The dough's in the fridge. We can always finish later…" Her voice trails, thick with lust as she looks me over. It's as if she's looking right through my clothes to picture me naked. It wouldn't be the first time.

"Okay." I nod, my cheeks burning. I think we're going to head to the bedroom, but she doesn't get off me and instead starts kissing my neck.

"Are we going to do it here?" I ask as she uses one hand to untie the apron.

"Yes. I want you right here. Right now," she murmurs as she nibbles on my earlobe.

Our flour-stained hands paw at each other with just as much hunger. She slides her legs over me so she can straddle me while she leans in for a kiss. I taste a bit of flour as our lips meet, and we both laugh. I grab her body, pulling her ass toward me as she grinds on me. Her tongue slips in my mouth, and I groan at the familiar taste. She's unbuttoning my top, and I can feel her fingertips brushing against the skin on my chest, making goose bumps appear. I tug at her T-shirt, pulling it over her head, thanking every god when I see she's not wearing a bra, and dip my head to attach my mouth to her nipple.

"Holy fuck." She moans, her head falling back as I suck harder.

I hum against her skin, my shirt getting tossed aside. Her skin is so soft, even smoother with the bit of flour still left on it. Her hands reach for my breasts, and she tugs on my nipples tightly. Groaning, I suck harder on hers. Rotating her hips, she grinds, trying to get more friction with my lower body, so I buck my hips toward her. I slide my hands into the back of her sweats and grab her ass through her panties. They're nothing special— just black cotton—but her tight ass is amazing.

Her tongue dances across my lips as she pulls me in for a kiss. I can't get enough of her lips, and I just want to keep kissing her as long as I possibly can. She slides off my lap and next to me on the floor. Our bodies rock against each other as she slides her leg between my thighs, and I groan. Her knee brushes against my pussy, and I want to risk everything to have her fuck me right now. She's kissing my neck, sucking gently. I wonder if she's going to leave a mark. But truthfully, I wouldn't care. It's not like I care if anyone else knows about us—or whatever the hell this is. This time we have to talk about things. We can't hook up for a third time without being adults about it. It's time to face the music and know where we stand once and for all.

Tilly unbuttons my jeans and tugs them off, letting them fall to the side of us. Clad in just my thong, my ass is freezing on the cool tile floor, but I'm not complaining. I'm overheated every-where else from Tilly. Her warm body and my skin are lava with how turned on I am from her. She pays my breasts attention, taking my nipples between her teeth and tugging roughly. Watching her green eyes gleam at me while she does is another level of hot. How the fuck am I supposed to think clearly when she looks at me like this? I can feel the desire dripping from her fingers. I've never had someone with this kind of want before. I know I'm soaked without her even touching my pussy—seeping through the very thin fabric of my thong. She reaches for my panties, but I move at the last second.

"I think we should take this to the bedroom—or at least wash our hands first," I say, pulling away. Stopping is the last thing I want to do, but with the food on our hands, I can't imagine that being good for our bodies.

"Shower?" Tilly's eyes twinkle. I nod, and she extends a hand as she stands up. This time I take it, letting her help me up off the floor.

"Do you remember where my bedroom is?" she asks.

"Yes?" I raise an eyebrow, and she smiles.

"Good. The door on the left is the bathroom. I'll be right behind you." She winks. Slapping my ass, I start up the stairs, and I can feel her eyes on my ass the whole time. Laughing, I race up the stairs, carrying my breasts so they don't hit me in the face. She's only seconds behind me, pulling my hand back into hers.

TWENTY-ONE

Tilly

As we make our way to the shower, her breasts sit on her stomach which is hanging over her panties. I love that she doesn't shy away from her curves—she owns them. They are a part of her, and she knows they are beautiful. You can tell that by the way she walks and carries herself. I watch her ass up the stairs, the thin sliver of black tucked between her ass cheeks. I can't wait to rip those off and have my way with her.

We make our way into the bathroom, and I reach in the shower to turn on the water. She had a good point; we're covered in flour, and neither one of us wants a yeast infection. Not exactly sexy, when you think about it. As the water heats up, I push her panties aside, letting the lace tear lightly so I can dip my fingers into her folds. She moans, her auburn hair cascading all around her as she tosses her head back in pleasure. Dropping to my knees, I can't help but ache for a taste. She puts one leg up on the side of the shower and I press my face between her thighs. I lick long, languid licks up and down her folds, tight circles around her clit and hold her by the waist to steady her. The last thing I'd want is her falling before we get to the good part.

"I want you to wrap those thighs around my head and let yourself come for me, baby," I command.

"Mmm, okay," she says breathlessly.

"I want to see you shaking before I stop," I murmur. Licking her pussy is good, but I want her to be begging to cum. So I reach up for her large breasts and play with her nipples. One hand inside her, pumping in and out while the other tugs and twists her nipples just hard enough to make her moan. God, when she moans it is godly.

"Oh my God!" she cries, and I know she's feeling more than she normally does.

I know she doesn't usually come with another person, but it 's a secret of mine that I'm dying to change that. The more I get to know her body, the more I want to have her finishing for me. She is definitely wet enough, so I think it's just about getting her out of her own head. I drop my hand from her body and look up at her.

"Get in the shower," I command.

"Y-yes." She nods and steps in the warm water. The whole bathroom is steamy from the water.

"I want to try something, but I need you to relax first, okay?" I look at her, waiting for her consent.

"Okay…" I can tell she's worried about what I'm going to do.

"Do you trust me?" I ask.

"I do…but if you're going to try to stick something in my butt, then I should let you know I definitely didn't prepare for that."

I laugh. "No, I'm not doing that."

She nods. I take the shower hose off the wall, and her eyes widen as I change the settings from a rainfall to a jet. I've used it on myself more than a few times, so I know how it feels, and I have a feeling this might be the thing to send Bells over the edge to come. I make sure the water isn't too hot before spraying it over her chest. She gasps at the contact of the warm water, and her nipples harden. I let the water hit each of them for a minute before moving down her stomach toward her core.

"Tell me how this feels," I say. I spray the water over her clit, and her eyes shut closed.

"Oh my God!" She grips the side of the shower as I let the water hit her clit.

"This seems like the time to make you beg for it," I joke.

"Mmm." She's breathless as I let the water spray her.

Switching hands, I use my free hand to slip inside her. Bells almost collapses into me, her hips bucking and her body shaking. She isn't used to this much sensation; I can tell by the goosebumps all over her skin. Her body is dripping wet, the stream of water only hitting her in one place while she fights for her life to stand up.

"Just relax…" I murmur into her skin as I lean in to kiss her neck.

She moans lightly in my ear as I suck softly on the side of her neck. Not hard enough to leave a mark, but enough to keep her moaning. The shower head is clearly doing its job, and I keep it steady.

"How does it feel, baby?" I don't know where the pet name comes from but it feels right in the moment.

"S-so good." She gasps.

"I want you to play with your breasts while I try something," I tell her.

She must trust me now that the shower head was on. Because her hands immediately jump to her chest and she squeezes and tugs on her breasts. Her eyes are still closed, but I can see how much she's chasing this release. It's the first time I've seen her this relaxed. So I slide my hands up the insides of her thighs and she moans. I slide two fingers through her slick folds before slipping them inside her. I curl them tightly, and she almost falls forward. I make sure to steady her before positioning the shower head back on her clit.

"I want to see how you let go," I murmur quietly.

"Oh, fuck! Tilly!" she cries out as I pump my fingers in and out of her.

Her pussy clutches my fingers tightly as the water from her clit drips down my hands. I'm starting to get a little chilly, but I'm so close to this, I know I can't stop. Watching Bells come undone might be the best thing I've ever witnessed. I keep a steady rhythm, making sure she's close. Studying her breathing and the way her stomach heaves in and out as I hit her G-spot just so as the shower head hits her clit.

"YES! RIGHT THERE!" she starts yelling. "Don't you dare stop!"

I wouldn't stop even if I could. Bells clenches her thighs together as she finishes, and I instantly feel proud of myself. That was the first time for us that she actually finished. She'sred, her hair stringy and wet all over her face, but she's never looked more beautiful.

"Wow," I mutter as she bats my hand away and I pull my fingers out.

"I know, holy shit. I can't recall the last time I actually finished with someone else." She gasps, gripping the side of the wall.

"Are you okay?" I pull the shower head away from her so she can have a second to relax.

"Yes, oh my God. Yes." She pulls me in for a kiss and I drop the shower head. The hose catching it from hitting the bottom of the tub, the water splashes everywhere. Thank God the curtain is closed or my entire bathroom would be soaked.

Pulling back, I switch the setting back to a gentle rainfall and slide the shower head back into the holder on the wall. Bells looks at me with red cheeks and a crooked smile. I grab a washcloth and wet it, pouring on a handful of soup before running it down her chest. I've never taken a shower with someone before, but I kind of assumed actually showering would be part of it. I turn the water up higher again, so it takes away some of our chill. Bells's skin is soft but covered in goose bumps. I take my time running the washcloth over her entire body, and then she reaches for mine to do the same.

I can feel her hand through the washcloth as she caresses each part of my skin. It feels more intimate than I anticipate—definitely more than it has been in the past. With her or anyone else, for that matter. I know in this moment that I can't keep quiet anymore. I don't just want to hook up with her—I want to have more of her. I want to see the parts that not everyone gets to see. I want to know all the things that she only tells to some.

I also know it means I have to pop the bubble we're living in and tell her how I feel. I'm sure we could continue on like this, like it's nothing—that it's just a hookup—but I can't.

For too long I've lived my life with countless one-night stands, and that has always been enough. But suddenly, I want to have more with her. It isn't just with anyone, and I'm sure if she doesn't feel the same way, I'll go back to my one-night stands. But with her, it makes me want to try being with her, for real.

"I think we should talk about this," I say quietly, as I drop the washcloth I'm using into her hands.

She spins around to face me, her hair sticking to her wet face, water droplets dripping down her cheeks. I smile looking at her. She was so fucking beautiful.

"Okay, what are you thinking?" she asks softly.

"I don't want to keep being your secret lay. I don't want to keep hooking up with you. I think I want to be something real with you. Take you on dates *and* hook up with you," I add to lighten the mood.

"I think I'd like that." She smiles.

"You would?" I can't hide my surprise.

"Yeah, I feel like there's something here and we shouldn't try to ignore that."

"I didn't know you felt that way," I admit.

"I don't think I was ready to admit it to myself." She blushes.

Instead of saying anything more, I kiss her. One of those

cliché romantic kisses where I pull her body into mine and we lose all sense of time. Her lips are soft and wet, our bodies still under the water running between us. I wrap my arms around her waist, and she twirls her fingers through my hair. We only pull back when the water starts to run cold. I step out first, grabbing a fresh towel from the closet and holding it open for her. She steps on the rug, dries off her legs and wraps it around herself. I follow her into the bedroom, after wrapping my towel around me.

"Do you have a big T-shirt or something I could borrow? Just to get home?" she asks.

"I probably do." I walk to my closet and then I pause, turning around to face her. "What if you stayed?"

"Huh?"

"Why don't you stay? Just go home in the morning or something," I suggest.

"Oh, I mean, I guess so. Sure." She nods.

"Here." I grab her a Sapphire Orchards T-shirt that is way too big on me so would probably fit her.

"Do you think we could have something to eat? I'm sort of starving," she admits shyly.

"Of course. I was going to make chicken cutlets for dinner, but if you prefer takeout, I'm happy to order something too," I suggest.

"I love chicken cutlets." She smiles. She slips the T-shirt over her head, and it fits her like a long T-shirt. Just covering her pussy and the tops of her thighs. I'm pretty sure if she bent over, I'd be able to see everything.

"Why don't you come hang out in the kitchen with me while I cook and we can watch a movie or something while we eat?" I ask.

"That sounds great." I throw on some clothes and follow her back downstairs.

TWENTY-TWO

Bells

"Wow, the pies look amazing!" Lina praises as Tilly and I unload them.

We set up the event in one of the empty field spaces with lots of folding tables and chairs, so all the participants have space. Everyone gets an apple pie, and whoever eats the fastest is going to win a $100 gift card to use at the orchard's gift shop or Lina's bakery.

"Why do you sound surprised?" Tilly asks.

"I didn't know how much pie making would actually be happening." Lina laughs.

Tilly and I exchange a glance. We didn't say anything to anyone, but it must be obvious. I guess if we aren't fighting, it's obvious something is going on between us.

"It's my first time making apple pies, but I'm very excited," I say.

"Do you think you'll join the contest?" Tilly asks.

"I don't think so. I mean, it's not like I'd win." I shrug.

"Benny used to join in just for the fun of it," Lina adds.

"Oh, hmm." I pause. "Maybe I should join in then. Do you do it?"

Tilly points at herself. "Me? No, I like pie, but I don't enjoy quickly eating. I'll get a stomachache."

"Gotcha." I nod.

Is this something you have to practice for? It seems pretty straightforward. Like you just stop whenever you feel full or don't want any more. So it doesn't seem like there's much of a catch. I'm curious to see what all the fuss is about, and I wouldn't mind eating one of the pies I made.

"I'll be right back. I need to get the rolls of paper towels for after." Tilly jogs back inside to Lina's bakery.

"You two seem to be getting along." Lina winks at me playfully.

"We finally talked, and I think we're going to actually try to see if it could be something." I smile.

Hattie is listening to us but not saying a word. She's someone I always have a tough time getting a read on. Her face isn't happy with this conversation, but I don't really know why. Maybe she's just overprotective of her friends seeing new people —especially someone who didn't come in with a great first impression.

"I'm so happy for you two!" Lina wraps her arms around me, and Hattie storms away.

"Is she okay?" I look at Lina, who frowns.

"I'll handle it." Lina takes off in Hattie's direction just as Tilly comes back with the paper towels.

"What'd you do to clear a room?" she jokes.

"Excuse me, I was talking to your friends about you. But Hattie got all weird and took off. Lina said it was okay, though." I explain.

Tilly makes a face, so I raise an eyebrow until she sighs.

"I wasn't going to say anything, and I hope you won't. But Hattie told me several months back that she had feelings for me. They were never reciprocated, and I don't even know if she still has them, but I guess she does." Tilly sighs.

"Well, now I feel like an idiot. I'm sorry. I definitely won't say a word."

It makes sense—I mean, Tilly is gorgeous, and they're best friends. It makes sense that the lines got blurred for her. It's not like you can fault someone for having feelings.

"Hey, Bells, sorry to interrupt, but people are starting to get here, and we don't know where to direct them," Timmy, one of the people I hired at the start of the season, says, running over. He's only twenty and has a bit of nervous energy when it comes to talking to me. But he does a good job, so I keep him around.

"I'll handle it. Follow me." I take the clipboard from him and start looking over the names of everyone participating in the pie-eating contest.

We have enough pies and tables set up—we just have to wrangle in the crowd so there isn't too much disarray when the event actually happens. I have Timmy rope off two areas near the contest, with a path down the middle. After the event, everyone is free to roam the orchard, so we have the tractor and trailer set up to transport anyone.

As everything gets settled, I grab the microphone I bought for purposes like this and try to get the crowd's attention.

"Hello, everyone! I'm Bells, the owner of Sapphire Falls Orchard! How's everyone doing today?"

The crowd cheers, and all the contestants are behind me getting ready to eat.

I go over a few quick rules and announcements before taking my own place at the end table. Tilly takes over on the microphone for me, and I hold my arms behind my back. Everyone has their body at a ninety-degree angle to be able to start eating as soon as possible. I try, but that isn't exactly possible with my belly and boobs in the way.

Tilly says go, and I start eating. It's a lot harder than I anticipate. My entire face is basically in the pie because if not, you can't gather enough in your mouth to actually eat any of it. I try to use my tongue to maneuver bigger pieces into my mouth, but most of it is stuck to my face. The gooey inside melts to my cheeks as the crust crumbles, sticking to the inside like glue. I'm chewing as fast as I can, but I get thirsty pretty quickly, and all I want is a sip of water.

I take a break just to take a breath, but then I'm back to eating the pie, and although this is a bit of a mess, I'm having fun. Everyone nearby is cheering us on while laughing. I wonder what I must look like right now. One of the social media interns I hired is getting content of everyone participating—including myself—so at least I'll get to see it all later.

"And we have a winner!" Tilly announces, and I'm grateful I can stop eating.

Everyone claps for the winner, a small child who looks like she weighs maybe forty pounds. I want to ask her how the hell she did it, but instead I'm hearing my name quietly whispered from nearby. I glance around as I wipe my face clear of any apple pie. Then my eyes lock on the woman who looks out of place.

In a pair of cheetah-print heels, a pencil skirt, and a pair of huge sunglasses, she looks like one of the Real Housewives—not my mother.

I make my way over to her. What the hell is she doing here? Is she about to tell me in front of everyone I have to sell her the orchard? What am I going to do?

I glance over at Tilly, who is too busy taking photos of the winner to be bothered by what I'm doing. I feel bad for keeping so much from Tilly, but she doesn't need to be in the middle of me and my family drama.

"Mom? What are you doing here?" I take another napkin off the table and wipe away the remains of the apple pie crumbs from my face.

"I thought I'd come check up on the place since you were in the city. But it turns out you've got things under control here, huh?" She takes her sunglasses off and crosses her arms over her chest.

"I don't understand. I told you I was handling everything." I pull her toward the empty barn to give us a bit of privacy.

"You're eating pie like a heathen and acting like this place isn't up for sale. What's going on?" She scowls at me.

"It's part of raising morale. I can't get sellers in here if it looks dead and like there's no foundation for using this place. You know the sales were terrible, so I come up once in a while to check on things. I'm not staying for long," I lie.

"Sales are better?" She looks happily surprised.

"They are. I took us out of the negatives, and now we're making a huge profit every week. It's all part of the plan. I know it takes time, but if we want to sell the place, then this is what we have to do." I sigh.

"I see. I was just surprised to find you here looking so chummy."

"I am their boss, even if they think I'm keeping the place. It's not like I could get everyone on board to sell if I didn't play nicely."

"Fine. But your father and I want this deal closed sooner rather than later. You've pulled it out of the negatives, so there's no reason for you to keep doing things. I expect to see a proposal and a statement of transfer in my inbox soon."

"You don't think we should take more time—"

She cuts me off. "More time for what? It's a waste to think there's anything more in this small town. Especially on this property." She wrinkles her nose in disgust.

"It's not that bad."

"Not that bad? Sweetheart, I'm going to have to toss these shoes in the garbage when I'm done here, and they're Prada. You can't seriously tell me you're enjoying yourself here."

She waits for me to say something. I know I should defend this place, but I don't have it in me. I know it isn't a fight I'm going to win—not against her.

"I just meant it's fine for the time being." I sigh.

"I just don't want you wasting your life up here like my sister did. She spent her whole life building this place just for her to die and then the place to almost fail around her."

"I don't think that's what happened..." I say quietly.

"Plus, it's about time you head back to the city. I know Taylor got that job you wanted, but frankly she was more qualified, and you need to focus your free time on finding someone to marry. You're almost thirty, and your prospects are getting smaller and smaller."

It's not the first time she's said something like this to me. It's always the same—something a mother shouldn't be saying to her child. She wants me to marry for money, even though that clearly didn't work out well for her. She's worried my age is a factor and thinks my prospects are dwindling. It's like I'll turn thirty and suddenly be unattainable to all people on the planet. Something that doesn't make much sense to me—but then again, most of the things out of my mother's mouth are outdated. And usually offensive.

"I really appreciate your visit, Mother, but I can assure you I'm doing okay." I sigh.

"Fine. I can take a hint. I'll expect to hear from you soon." She puts her oversized sunglasses back on and shakes her head disapprovingly at me before heading out of the barn.

Sighing, I take a moment before I go back to the crowd. I take some deep breaths in and out until I feel calmer. Every time I see my mother, I feel like I need a long nap and a stiff drink. Something about my family just makes me want to run away to a beach somewhere far away and live there. But knowing them, they'd find me just to tell me I was doing something wrong. For people who always have something negative to say about how you're living your life, they have a tendency to stay in your life.

I don't know why I let them stick around—probably because she's my mother. Even though at this point that means very little to me unless you're talking about genetics.

TWENTY-THREE

Tilly

"What's the matter with you? You look like you've seen a ghost," Hattie says as I stomp back to the bakery where she and Lina are hanging out.

"I-I just overheard Bells say to her mother that she's selling the place." I can't even believe the words I'm saying. If I didn't hear it myself, I wouldn't believe it.

"What?" Lina and Hattie ask in unison.

"I need a drink," I grumble.

Lina hands me a bottle of water. "I can offer you a coffee, but that's about the strongest thing in here."

"What exactly did she say?" Hattie asks.

"Her and her mom were talking, and her mom was basically like, why are you still here? When are we selling the place? And she wanted the timeline of the sale moved up," I explain.

"This doesn't make any sense." Lina frowns.

"I mean, we don't know her that well. Maybe it's true." Hattie says.

"I just don't get it. I asked her, I've said it for months. Why wouldn't she just tell us if she was selling the place?" I say angrily.

"Can you afford to buy it?" Lina asks, eyes sparking with hope.

"No. I mean, maybe if I was given a deal and some time, but they want big money for this place and that's something I just don't have." I sigh. I need something short of a miracle to have enough money for this place.

"Did you try talking to Bells?" Lina asks.

"No, I sort of overheard and then ran over here," I admit sheepishly.

"So is it possible maybe you misunderstood?" Lina asks.

"I mean, sure. But it wasn't exactly a hushed conversation. I don't think I misunderstood what they were saying, I'm just not understanding why Bells has been lying to us." I sigh.

"Lying about what?" Bells voice sneaks up behind us and my jaw drops.

"We'll give you two a moment," Lina says, ushering her and Hattie out of the shop.

"Lying about what?" Bells asks again.

"I overheard you and your mother."

"Oh." She frowns.

"Oh? That's all you have to say."

"Look, she comes across harsh but don't take anything she says to heart. She's not exactly the warm and fuzzy type." Bells sighs.

"Are you defending her?"

"No, I'm just saying. She makes everything seem more complicated than it is. There's no pressure on us or whatever this is. It's not like I'm ready to get married."

"What?!" Now I'm confused.

"What? You said you heard us." She looks at me with furrowed brows.

"Yeah, talking about selling the orchard," I say.

"Oh." Her eyes widen.

"She wants you to get married? Us to get married?" I felt the urge to run. I liked Bells but I was nowhere near ready for marriage.

"No, she wants me to think about it. She doesn't know anything about you or us. It's just something she pushes on me, and I usually ignore her," Bells explains.

"But you're selling the orchard?" My voice cracks as I ask because I'm too afraid to hear if that's true or not.

"No." Bells takes my hands in hers, but I don't relax. "My mother thinks I am, it's complicated family drama which I'm sure is why Aunt Blake left the place to me. But no, I'm not selling it."

"Really?" I feel the anxiety seeping back inside.

"When I first got here, I thought maybe I'd sell it. I didn't know what to do or how to run anything. I took a look at the books, and this place was in danger of being foreclosed. So I've done everything I can to keep that from happening," she explains.

"Wait, it wasn't making a profit?" This confuses me. I always thought we were doing well.

"The maintenance on this place, as well as other factors, were hemorrhaging this place. I just got it out of the red and back to making money. Before I got to know this place, I thought maybe I'd fix it up to sell—to someone who would keep everyone's jobs and keep the place as is. But now I know I don't want to sell it at all." She smiles.

"How come?" I ask.

"Because this place is like a home to me now. I love the city, and I'm sure I'll visit, but something about this found family we have here—everyone working together, all the opportunities to try new things and use my business degree for something new— it's really lifted my spirits and made me feel good again."

I can't describe the relief I feel. My stomach goes from panicking to relaxing in a matter of minutes. Bells thinks this place feels like family? I know that's how I feel, but I didn't realize this place was growing on her as much as it has.

"I really like you, City Girl." I smile.

"We're bringing back the nicknames?! I really like you too, Mac." She laughs. "Wait! Is that a reference to McIntosh apples?!"

"Yes." I chuckle. "I was wondering when you might realize that."

"You gave me a hint to who you were all along. I didn't even realize it." She laughs.

"I don't want you to feel any pressure here, but if you want to talk about things with your mom, you can. It seemed pretty intense from what I heard," I admit.

"It's just how she is. Lately it's getting harder and harder to defend. I'm starting to realize why Aunt Blake moved out here and never looked back. It's a lot easier than dealing with the family all the time." She sighs.

"I'm not telling you what to do, but is that something you ever consider? Maybe it would give you some peace, cutting ties."

"Is that what you did? With your family?" she asks.

"It's a little different. I told them who I was—that I like women—and they kicked me out. All ties severed for life. I don't even know where they are or how they've been. I'm not saying it's easy. But I do know it's better than the alternative of living the rest of my life hiding who I am."

"That makes sense. I mean, my mother ironically approves of me being with women—it's just anything else I possibly do that's the problem."

"I see. I'm sorry. I know family issues aren't easy."

Bells takes a deep breath and then looks at me. "I just feel like whatever I do, it won't be enough. And not in the typical my-parents-will-never-be-proud-of-me way, but in the sense that there's always something they're going to complain about. I managed to turn this whole place around without any of their money or help, but they still treat me like I don't know anything. They want to take this place and probably charge twenty bucks an apple and make it more of an amusement park to bring in revenue. I don't want any of that. I just don't know how to show them this place is so much more."

"Why do you have to show them?" I ask. "I mean, I understand why you'd want to. But what if it's just something they won't understand?"

"You have a point. I don't know. I guess it's because they're my parents. But it's also because they're my parents that I know they won't change." She sighs.

"You're very similar to Benny, just so you know," I say quietly. I don't know how she might take this.

"Really?" She perks up next to me.

"She always wanted to make peace with your family. Talked about how one day she hoped they'd come around and see this place for more than a quick buck. She had the same drive you have about this place. It's really amazing to get to witness."

Her face lights up. "I have to show you something!" Suddenly pulling my hand, she drags me out of the bakery.

"Where are we going?" I ask, but she doesn't answer.

She's holding my hand tightly and pulling us toward the houses. I assume she's bringing me to her house for some reason, but I honestly can't begin to guess what it is. She unlocks her front door and finally lets go of my hand.

"Wait right here." She tells me before running upstairs.

"What?" I search for a clue of what's going on, but she's already gone. A few minutes later, she returns with an envelope with my name on it. The handwriting is familiar, but I just can't place it.

"I found this a little while back, and I'm sorry for not giving it to you earlier. I needed to figure this place out before you knew the truth about the orchard being in debt. But this is from Aunt Blake." Bells hands me the envelope, and my heart drops.

"She left you this in the will?" I ask, my eyes brimming with tears.

"No, they were among her things. There's one for Hattie and

Lina too. I didn't know why she didn't just give them to you, so I did read them. And I can understand if you're upset with me for keeping them. But it was always my intention to give them to you once you knew about the orchard."

I take the envelope from her, tracing my fingers over the black ink of my name. Carefully sliding the piece of paper out, I begin to read her note.

Dear Tilly,

I regret having to write this, and I hope things may change before I give you this. I know I've promised you the orchard. I think you would do amazing things with it, and you would keep my vision alive for years and years to come. You'd make this a safe haven for all those who need it, just like I did for you. But at this point in time, I know I cannot leave it to you. We're not making a profit, and I'm afraid things are going downhill. With my diagnosis, I fear things will only get worse instead of better. You are destined for such amazing things, and I don't want you tied to my failure. This is why I've decided to leave the orchard to my niece, Arabella. She has done amazing things working for non-profits and volunteering for underprivileged and queer youth. She will know how to get us out of this hole. And if not, she will sell the place to someone who can. I know this is not what you want to hear. And I'm sorry if you're angry about it—I completely understand. But please know this is for your best interest. I do not want you tied to such a huge loss so early on in your career.

You have made this orchard less of a job and more of a home. I never intended to take you in, let alone Hattie and Ollie, and Lina too, but I'm so glad I did. You four became my family in ways only you understand. My own family has always had their own challenges, and I've never connected with them the way we did. I will treasure our time together, and I hope you come to understand my reasoning. Thank you for being true to yourself and authentic in all the ways I was never brave enough to be.

• • •

Love,
   Benny

By the end, I'm crying, and Bells is offering me a tissue from the box. All this time, I thought Benny didn't believe in me or thought I wasn't good enough to run this place. But it turns out she was just trying to protect me. She didn't want me to have more stress about getting the orchard out of debt and it effecting the rest of my life. I can't begin to explain the amount of relief I feel just knowing this is the truth. Sure, I wish I knew a little earlier, but even knowing now makes things better.

TWENTY-FOUR

Bells

It's the first time I've ever seen Tilly cry, and I don't entirely know what to do. So besides offering her a tissue, I extend my arms in case she wants a hug. I won't be offended if she doesn't. Everyone has different needs when they're upset. But Tilly accepts my hug and leans into my chest to cry. I rub small circles on her back and wonder if it was the best idea now to give her the letter. Maybe she would've been happier not knowing?

"I'm sorry if you think I shouldn't have given you the letter. I thought you'd want it, but I should've asked." I sigh.

"No! I'm not crying about the letter. Well, I am. But not in the way you think." I give her a chance to blow her nose and then she continues. "I really thought she left you this place because she thought I couldn't handle it. And that's part of why I hated you so much. She barely knew you, but she thought you'd do a better job than I could. It didn't make any sense. I spent my life working for this. But now knowing it wasn't about me at all, and she was just trying to protect me. It makes me feel a lot of things."

"I didn't know you thought that. I thought you were just mad she left it to me."

"Well yeah, but it was mostly because of my feelings attached to it. Like I thought she suddenly thought less of me or something. But clearly, she was right in her choice. You turned this place around and saved it. In a lot of ways I never thought were possible." She smiles.

"I guess Aunt Blake kept up on me. She had all these notes about me and why I'd be the best for the job. It was jarring but I'm hoping I made her proud," I admit.

"You definitely did."

"I do want to ask you something. Now that this place is in the green again, would you be interested in being my co-owner? I don't want to give this place up, but I'd be willing to share it with you." I smile. It's something I'd been thinking about for the last few weeks.

"Really?" Her face lights up.

"Yeah, I can't guarantee whatever this is will work out with us. I hope it does, don't get me wrong. But either way, I hope you'll be my business partner and keep my aunt's legacy alive."

"I would love that." She nods. "But I'd also like you to be my romantic partner too."

"I think we might be able to arrange that," I tease with a wink.

Tilly leans in to kiss me, her lips soft and tender. Her cheeks are dry from any tears, so I hold them in my hands as I kiss her. She tugs gently on my bottom lip with her teeth, and I moan. Her tongue slips in, and she pulls my body into hers. Tilly takes her time kissing me. Nothing about this is rushed despite the fact that I can feel the need growing between us. I palm her breasts through her T-shirt, and she tugs at the bottom of my shirt. I want to yell at her to take it off and fuck me, but I restrain myself. I want this moment to last between us. Plus, I usually liked to be the one making her beg, not doing the begging.

Tilly's mouth starts trailing down my neck. She grabs my breasts in her hands and plays with them gently. She slides up my shirt painfully slow and then dips her head to my chest, taking my nipple in her mouth. She glides her teeth over it, taking the time to suck. My thighs clench together as she switches between each one.

"Please, touch me. More," I finally beg.

"I thought you'd never ask." She smirks and slides her tongue down my stomach.

Tilly stops just above the waistband of my clearly soaked panties. I can smell my arousal from here, so God only knows what she's thinking. She presses her thumb to the wet spot on my clit, and my hips buck toward her involuntarily.

"Oh, fuck!" I moan.

"God, you're so needy." Her eyes are dark with desire.

Tilly tugs my panties to the side and slides a finger down the lips of my pussy. I bite back a moan as I shiver again. She is touching my aching pussy, and I love it. Oh, I am *definitely* into this woman.

"I'm going to fuck you now, okay?" Tilly looks up at me.

"Yes, please," I say with a heavy breath.

She slides down my soaked panties and tosses them aside. I watch as she looks at my pussy with desire. Tilly presses her tongue to my clit, and I moan effortlessly for her. She slides her tongue through my pussy, lapping up all of me, and I can't hold back my moans. Tilly is taking her time with me, and I'm enjoying every second of it. She knows my body so well at this point, knowing it takes me longer than most to finish. That I like to lather up all the foreplay I can get.

She stops for a moment to free my breasts, tossing aside my shirt and bra. Only to return to between my thighs and press her face to my pussy. My breath hitches as she makes contact with my clit. She sucks on it lightly, lighter than she did to my nipples, and then swirls her tongue down my pussy. I reach for her head and grip her hair tightly as she presses her tongue to my clit again. She's paying close attention to my reactions, and I'm able to relax under her touch.

"Mm, yes! Suck right there," I encourage her when she returns to sucking on my clit.

She drags a finger up my pussy and easily slides it inside me. "C-can you add another finger?" I moan.

She nods, looking up at me, but between my belly rolls and me holding her hair, I can't see very much below me. She removes her fingers to add a second one, slowly teasing me inside. She curls them just like she did in the shower, and I can feel my orgasm rising.

"Tilly! I'm gonna cum!" I cry loudly.

"Come for me, baby," she tells me and moves her tongue even faster on my clit.

She sucks down hard on my clit, and I see fucking stars. I didn't know an orgasm with another person could feel that fucking good. Holy hell. I collapse into the couch we're on and she places soft kisses along my thighs and pubic bone.

"I'm s-so sensitive," I mutter.

"Want me to stop?" she asks with a smirk.

"Just for now," I admit.

She leans on the side of the couch and pulls my body closer to her. We're a mess, I'm completely naked and she's still fully clothed but I was in heaven. She kisses my forehead, and I can smell myself on her.

"I love making you cum," she murmurs in my ear.

"I'm a fan," I say lazily.

She places a hand on my cheek and smiles. "You're beautiful."

"So are you." I smile but she makes a face. "I mean it. I feel so lucky to be with someone so beautiful."

"Come on," she groans.

"I'm serious." I stare at her until a blush creeps across her cheeks.

She kisses me, this time with more tension. Climbing on top of me, she tears off her T-shirt. She catches me staring as she unhooks her bra and tosses it aside.

"Like what you see?" she asks, smirking.

"Oh yes," I murmur and take her boobs in my hands. I slide my hands down her chest and around her waist, down to her ass, pulling her against me.

I bend down to take a nipple in my mouth between my teeth.

"Oh, fuck!" she calls out, gasping.

I flick my tongue over each nipple several times until she's squirming against me. Then I place delicate kisses up her chest and down her neck and over again until she's squirming.

"Can I fuck you?" I ask quietly as I look up at her.

"Yes, please," she says excitedly.

She climbs off me to take off her pants, dropping them to the ground, and this time I'm the one on top. "You still don't want to be eaten out?" I ask.

"Honestly, I'm not opposed right now," she whispers, biting her bottom lip.

That's all I needed to know. I dip my head toward her glistening, wet pussy and slide my tongue over her clit. She responds immediately, bucking her hips toward my face. I soak in every drop of her sweet juices, and I only want more. Fuck, how did I go this long without knowing how good she tastes? I wish she would've let me do this months ago. I hope she'll let me do this again. I flatten my tongue against her core and sop up every drip of her. She pushes my head down closer to her clit, and I suck gently on her sensitive bud. Her thighs clasp around my head tightly, like earmuffs, and I flick my tongue over her clit.

"Oh, fuck. Bells, don't stop," she moans out. I can barely hear her with her thighs around me, but I make out her heavy pants.

I hum against her, and she goes wild. Her hand tangles itself in my hair, and I lick harder and faster for her. I can feel her body getting closer and closer to orgasm the more I lick. I just want her to come for me. I want to know what she sounds and feels like when she lets go and explodes all over me. I slide one finger into her dripping pussy, and she screams in pleasure.

"YES!"

I curl my finger inside her, feeding off her reactions, and she is so close it must be painful. So I pump my finger in and out of her pussy while I suck on her clit, and I can feel her stomach raising with each deep breath. It's only seconds before she's screaming my name and coming all over my face. I soak up every last drop of her juices as her pussy contracts, and I give her one last lick. Her thighs go limp, letting me free, and I look at my girl that's clearly spent from her orgasm.

"Holy fuck." She gasps breathlessly as I wipe my mouth dry.

"That good?" I tease.

"I'll definitely be asking you to do that again." She moans again. "As long as you want to," she adds quickly.

"Oh, yes please. I can think of a few different ways I'd like to do that." I wink.

"First, we need to get something to eat, because God, you taste and small like apple pie. I've been craving it since you kissed me. So please tell me we saved a pie somewhere," Tilly says and I start laughing.

"I think you left one around, want me to check the kitchen?" I go to move off the couch, but Tilly pulls me back down.

"Not yet. I just want to lay with you first." She wraps her arms around my naked body, we pull a blanket over us, and we both relax.

I can't help but think about my aunt in this moment and how grief changed the course of my life. I can no longer imagine my world without Tilly—or without the orchard. For the first time in a long time, I feel at peace here, surrounded by my little makeshift family and someone I care so deeply about. My mind races with a hundred new ideas for this place, but I don't leap up to write them down. There's no rush. I have time—years and years, I hope—to bring them to life.

Epilogue I

BELLS

It's late October and while the orchard is mostly done with apple and pumpkin picking, we've transferred to other fall activities. Today is our first of several fall weddings for the next several weekends. I had put out feelers, wanting to know if there was an interest in couples getting married here and our form was overflowing with responses within hours. Apparently the orchard was the perfect fall backdrop for engagement photos and wedding receptions.

"Did the bridesmaids bouquets arrive okay?" One of the wedding planners asks.

"Yup, they're in the cooler so they don't wilt before the ceremony." I smile.

"Perfect!" She saunters off to check on more details while I check off my to do list.

"Hey, I was looking for you." Tilly smiles as she catches my arm. She's holding a tray with two lattes in her other hand.

"Thank you, I completely forgot to have breakfast." I admit.

"I know, which is why I grabbed one of these as well." She pulls out a fresh croissant in a paper wrapper from her back pocket.

I laugh, "Keeping it warm back there?"

"I didn't have another hand." She laughs. "Everything going okay?"

Tilly looks around, taking in the space. It looked exactly like the mood boards we helped the clients put together. The colors were dark orange and auburn, melting beautifully into the natural colors of the trees changing. The bride was wearing a traditional white dress but the groom was also wearing white so their outfits would pop against the autumn scenery.

"Looks like everything we planned." Tilly says answering her own question.

I take a sip of the pumpkin latte she got me and I melt. I would have to ask Lina if this is something we could have year round.

"Do you ever think about getting married?" Tilly asks and I almost drop my latte. My eyes must show it because she quickly adds, "Not right now! I just meant in general. To be clear I was not proposing."

I laugh, watching her flail over her anxiety was cute as heck. "Yes, I do think about getting married. I know I'm almost thirty and my parents think about it way more than I do, but I'm not in any rush. I'd rather wait and make sure I only get married once."

"That makes sense, I feel like I'd be fine either way. Like if my partner wants to I'd get married, but if they didn't want to I'd also be okay." Tilly explains.

"I get it, there's way too much pressure these days to get married when I'm not sure how much it actually changes except stuff for your taxes." I joke.

"Pretty sure our taxes are a pain in the ass next year anyway now that we're owning an orchard." Tilly adds.

"Excuse me, do you know where I can find the bride?" A dark haired woman asks with a camera around her neck.

"You are...?" I remember meeting her but her name was failing me right now. I wanted to make sure I wasn't letting some upset ex through to the bride.

"Sorry, I'm Max. The photographer, we met a few months ago when I did their engagement shoot here, but don't feel bad if you forgot. I'm used to people seeing the camera, not me." She jokes.

"I'm so sorry, today's a busy day. But yes, the bridal suite is right through there and I'm Bells if you need anything else." I smile shaking Max's hand.

"Tilly? Bells? There's guests arriving but I know it's a little early, is there something we should be doing?" One of our assistants asks over the walkie talkie's we have. Sometimes the cell service could be spotty up here and it was easier this way.

"I'll handle it, can you walk Max to the bridal suite?" I ask Tilly.

"Sure, but babe just relax. It'll all work out." Tilly smiles and briefly touches my arm to reassure me. I take a deep breath before I take a trek to the gates to welcome anyone who's here early.

"Arabella? Is this your doing?" I stop in my tracks as I see both my parents being held at the gates.

"I'm sorry, do you know them? I just assumed they were here for the wedding." Our assistant, Lisha says.

"They're my parents, you can let them through. But anyone else should be from the wedding." I tell Lisha. "What are you guys doing here?"

"We have the paperwork from the lawyers for you to sign, I didn't know there was a wedding going on. Who in their right mind would want to get married here?" My mother says, her face twisting in disgust.

"Come with me." I say, sighing. There was no way I was signing those papers but there was also no way I could have this conversation out here.

I lead them to the back of the empty storage hall. My parents look around in disgust and I know in about five seconds they're going to be looking at me that way. But I also knew it was going to be worth it.

"I'm not interested in selling the orchard and I will not be signing those papers." I tell them sternly.

"What?" Both of their jaws drop.

"This was your idea, how could you back out of it like this?" My father asks.

"It's not my idea. It was the family's idea and frankly I'm not interested in what the family wants to do. I turned this place around and we're making an actual profit so I'm going to keep this place running." I explain.

"You're going to keep it running?" My mother laughs.

"That's rich! What do you know about running an orchard?" My father adds in.

"I know enough, and my co-partner has been teaching me everything else I need to know." I say crossing my arms over my chest.

"Your co-partner? So one of these farmies talked you into keeping the place? Of course, that makes more sense." My mother scoffs.

"It's not feasible for you to keep this place." My father says seriously.

"I'm not quite sure why you think that since it's not like you've seen the finances of the place. We've been doing incredibly well for ourselves and we're only on target to exceed our expected goals for the quarter." I say confidently. I've been looking at the numbers and it wasn't like I was about to let this place suffer.

"Sweetheart, you've been here for less than six months. I understand you think you can handle this, but it's much more complicated than you think." My mother says in the most condescending done.

"I appreciate your thoughts, but frankly I didn't ask. I've already told you I'm not interested in selling or signing the papers today so if there's nothing else…"

"You might change your mind and the place won't be so lucrative then." My father says angrily.

"Then that will be a problem I'll have to figure out, and I will figure it out." I say sternly.

"Fine, then I guess we have no other reason to spend another moment here." My mother says in a huff.

"No problem, I have a wedding to get back to." I shake off the feelings of my parents not wanting to stay for me. I knew all along what they were really here for. I'd unpack those later, I didn't want them getting in the way of me doing my job.

My parents take off and I head back for the wedding, only stopping once to will away the tears that were threatening to come. I didn't have time right now to stop and redo my makeup. On the way back, I run into Tilly, literally.

"Fuck!" My chest slams into Tilly's and she catches me by the waist.

"Are you okay?" She asks stopping to look at me.

"I'm fine, I'm sorry. My parents were here and I wasn't thinking. I have to get to the—"

"Wait, your parents were here?" Tilly stops, cutting me off.

"Oh, yeah but it's—" I'm about to say it's fine when she holds her hands in my face. Which of course causes all the tears I've been holding back to fall. "My parents wanted me to sign the paperwork releasing the orchard over to them, but I said no. And I'm pretty sure that's the last time I'll see them because in their eyes I disappointed them."

"I'm so sorry babe." She tilts her head looking solemnly at me.

"It's okay, I'm fine. I just want to get through today and—"

"I can handle today if you need the day." Tilly says.

"I know you can, but trust me I'd rather be working. We can talk it out later, but for now I want to be working." I decide.

"Okay, then today we work and I don't ask if you're okay, but you can tell me if you aren't. And as soon as the day is through you come over for a hot bath, apple cider donuts and a twilight marathon at my place." Tilly says with a smile.

"I love the sound of that." I smile.

Tilly leans in to kiss me, hands me a tissue to clean up my face and we head into the wedding together. Making me feel like I can accomplish anything, with Tilly by my side.

Epilogue II

TILLY

After spending the night with Bells, I wake up in her bed. She's naked, tied up in her sheets her hair in disarray all around her. I smile, touching her cheek softly as I pull the sheet a bit more over her body. She's got goosebumps, the morning is much chillier than when we went to bed last night. Fresh out of the bath, we binged the first three twilight movies before she fell asleep in my arms.

I was so proud of her for standing up to her family like that. I know it wasn't easy, especially considering how selling the orchard is how she ended up here in the first place. I'm so relieved knowing this place grew on her and she's not the "city girl" I originally thought her to be. She reminds me so much of Benny in all of the best ways. I wish they could've known each other when Bells was older. But I guess everything was meant to happen, happened.

I hate skipping out on Bells, but I had a million things to do that I put on the back burner last night so I could take care of her. I write her a quick note, letting her know I'll be at the barn or at Lina's and leave it on her nightstand. I didn't want her to worry about me or feel left behind.

I get dressed in last nights clothes, thankful I didn't have to worry about seeing anyone on my short walk to the barn. I slip out the back of Bells' house and head right to the barn. I make sure everyone's fed and accounted for before I let them out to run around for the day. It's still beautiful weather so I didn't have to lock up for the winter yet. That's when we move them to the larger, winterized barn on the other side of the orchard. It was a bit of a pain when it came to feeding them but it was obviously safer for them.

As I finish up, I take the longer way out to my house. I needed a shower and to grab some breakfast before I head back to Bells' place. I'm walking back, thinking about texting Lina my order so I can just grab it when I see someone on Hattie's porch. I can't see them exactly, but assuming it's Hattie I walk over to say good morning and check in on things. To my surprise it's a man standing on the porch. A man, I definitely don't recognize.

"Can I help you?" I ask the man standing on Hattie's porch.

"I hope so, I'm looking for Hattie and Ollie." He says with a smile.

"Do you mind if I ask who exactly you are?" I tilt my head at him. He had shaggy blonde hair, but dark chocolate eyes that looked somewhat familiar.

"Right, sorry. I've been driving for the last few hours and I completely lost all my manners. My mother would kill me if she knew." He laughs. "I'm Christopher Black, I'm Ollie's father." He extends his hand and I'm mid shake by the time he finishes his sentence.

"You're..." My jaw drops.

"I've been gone for awhile, so I can understand why you might not know me. Do you work on the orchard or something?" Christopher asks. Now I knew why his dark eyes looked so familiar, they were Ollie's.

"I'm Tilly, Hattie is my best friend." I say a little sharply.

"Ah, probably not too thrilled to see me then. Understandably so, but I'm here to make things right. Have you seen them?" Christopher looks around.

"Chris?" Hattie appears behind us holding Ollie's hand tightly.

"Hattie! I was worried you weren't home! Ollie my goodness, you got so big!" Christopher smiles as Hattie freezes.

"What are you doing here?" She asks sharply.

"Why don't I take Ollie inside? Give you guys a chance to chat?" I suggest. I didn't know how this was going to go and I knew Hattie wouldn't want Ollie in the middle of it.

"Good idea." Hattie says at the same moment Christopher frowns at me. Ignoring that, I grab the key from Hattie and usher Ollie past his father and inside the house.

"Who was that guy?" Ollie asks quietly and I sigh, unsure of what to say to him. It wasn't my place to explain anything.

"I'm not sure, why don't we play? We can give your mother a moment to talk to him." I suggest.

"Alright." Ollie was pretty agreeable so I wasn't surprised when he heads for the playroom.

I glance out the front window, making sure Hattie was okay. Not that I thought he'd do anything, she never really talked about Ollie's father. So I didn't know what we were dealing with here. I'm about to join Ollie in the playroom when I see a brunette emerge from the car nearby. She was all legs, with cherry red lipstick and a shiny engagement ring on her left hand. She joins Christopher and Hattie on the porch. But who was she?

BELLS

There is nothing hotter than watching my girl work out. And by work out, I mean doing her job. She's out there right now, wearing a sports bra and a pair of jogging shorts as she moves hay bales around the backyard. I don't know her exact plan but she's determined to get all of them from one side of the backyard to the other. She's dripping in sweat and sex appeal, her blonde hair slicked back inside a red baseball cap with the orchard's logo. Her abs are on full display, tightly twisting and contorting with each bale of hay she drops. She stops to wipe her forehead off and take a sip of water. I find myself literally drooling at the sight of her.

I just finished moving the last of Benny's boxes from the attic and I was in need of a shower. As I walk across the house to the bathroom, I peek out the back window and realize I can still see Tilly. I tear off my shirt, letting my breasts hang free and open the window. Tilly's too busy working to notice, but I lean on the edge of the bathtub and realize this would be the perfect place to keep watching her. I kick my shorts and panties off to the side and take a seat on the cool porcelain side of the tub.

I lean my back against the tile wall and slide my hands down my chest. I grab my breasts, taking my nipples in between my fingers and tugging tightly. A small moan escapes my lips and I feel the heat growing between my legs. I slide my hand down my body and brush gently across my clit. A larger moan escapes my lips as I keep an eye on Tilly. Her body was so amazing to look at, fueling my sexual daydream. But as I slide two fingers through the wetness growing my head falls back and I moan louder.

"Oh fuck me, Tilly." I gasp as I slide two fingers inside me.

"Bells?" Hearing my name causes me to gasp.

I jump up, looking out the window at Tilly staring up at me in confusion, then her eyes getting wide. As she realizes I'm topless, her eyes widen and then looks at me even more confused.

"Hey babe!" I call out, deciding to take the moment and tease her.

"Uh hey Bells," She calls back cautiously.

"I'm just about to shower, saw my beautiful girlfriend working out and I thought I'd say hi." I hold up my boobs because although bigger, gravity hasn't been as nice to me as they were Tilly.

"Well, hello." She's standing in the backyard and I wonder if I should continue and give her a show or stop.

I stand a little taller, keeping my breasts perched on the window sill and sliding my hands back down to my pussy. As I slide two fingers inside myself, I whimper and Tilly is staring at me in absolute awe.

"Do you know what you're doing to me right now Arabella Kennedy?" Tilly says all commanding.

"Maybe I want you to come show me?" I smirk and Tilly comes barreling toward the house.

We have a habit of leaving our front doors unlocked these days. It wasn't like anyone came on the property and the second someone did, it wasn't to this part of the orchard either. So I'm not too worried when I hear my front door unlocking and footsteps running up the stairs. I close the window in the bathroom and open the bathroom door just in time to see Tilly stripping for me. Her shorts are on the ground, and her sports bra is in her hand.

"Holy shit that was quick." I laugh.

"You don't have to tell me twice." She pulls me in for a kiss and I moan.

She's salty, her soft lips tasting more like the ocean than normal. She pulls her hot body against mine, and I mean that literally. I'd think she was feverish if I didn't just see her outside. Her tits press into mine and I can feel her perky nipples against my smooth skin. Her lips are on my neck and I groan into her ear. Oh, I am definitely glad I opened that window for her.

"Let's get in the shower." I decide before she drops to her knees. I didn't want her tasting me like this.

"Mmm," She hums against my skin, climbing in behind me.

I turn on the cool water, letting it run warm for us and she picks up my washcloth. I grab hers, since she's here so often and we take turns cleaning the other. Her hands take their time over my breasts, my nipples sensitive to her delicate touch. My pussy aching to be more than touched each time she grazes by it. Each time we touch the other it feels like ecstasy, our bodies getting ready for more.

"I want you baby." She murmurs in my ear.

Rinsing off all the soap, I know we're clean enough to get dirty again. She smirks and pushes me back to leaning on the edge of the tub.

"Is this where you were? Touching yourself for me?" She looks at me with darkened eyes.

"Yes. I was so turned on watching you work." I admit, biting my bottom lip.

"Show me." She commands.

Tilly uses her hands to spread my thighs apart and leads my hand to my pussy. I brush my fingers over my aching clit as Tilly stares at me. I glide my fingers through the wetness she created and slip two fingers inside me, causing light moans. My eyes close, and she tips my head back.

"Uh uh, I want you to look at me while you touch yourself." She commands.

I nod, forcing my eyes open no matter how much I want to close them. She touches my chest, playing with my nipples and sucking on each of them. Taking one between her teeth while the other is in her hands. I use my thumb to touch my clit as the two fingers inside me curl inward. Tilly looks so fucking hot when she's touching me. Her body is absolute perfection and the way I want to ride her face right now is insane. The heat in my stomach grows hotter as I get closer to finishing. Just as I'm about to tell Tilly I'm going to cum, she pushes my hands out of the way and drops to her knees.

"I want a taste." In this moment I don't give a fuck what I taste like because her tongue is ungodly.

"Oh fuck!" I'm grabbing her hair, tugging on for dear life as she looks up at me with a mischievous smirk.

She hums against me and I whimper, she sucks on my clit and the pressure is too much for me. I suddenly feel like I'm going to pee and I want to push her away but I don't have a chance to. The pressure is too much and I'm screaming Tilly's name.

"Tilly! Yes! Yes! Yes!" My head hits the back wall and I'm breathless until she pulls away. "I'm so sorry, I think I might've peed. Which I didn't even know was a thing and that's so embarrassing—"

Tilly cuts me off with a wicked smile, "Babe, you didn't pee on me. You fucking squirted for me. All over my face and it was hot as fuck."

"Oh." My cheeks redden. "I've never done that before." I admit.

"Well, it's definitely something you'll be doing again." She licks her bottom lip and I shudder.

"Really?" I squeeze my thighs together. I was buzzing from the orgasm.

"Oh fuck yes, that was hot as hell." She pulls me in for a kiss and I relax under her touch.

I can taste myself on her as she slips her tongue in my mouth. It's only then I notice the shower's gone cold and Tilly's covered in goosebumps.

"Why don't we finish this in the bedroom?" I suggest.

"Only if you promise to let me try to do that again."

"Might be a little messier in the bedroom…"

"So? I promise to clean all of it up with my tongue." Tilly whispers as she licks down the side of my neck.

"Mm, then what are we waiting for?" I turn the shower off, and grab our towels. Tilly races behind me to the bedroom and the towels are dropped just as quickly.

Also by Shannon O'Connor

SEASONS OF SEASIDE SERIES

(each book can be read as a standalone)

Only for the Summer

Only for Convenience

Only for the Holidays

Only to Save You

Seasons of Seaside: The Complete Collection

LIGHTHOUSE LOVERS

(each book can be read as a standalone)

Tour of Love

Hate to Love You

To Be Loved

Inn Love

Love, Unexpected

ETERNAL PORT VALLEY SERIES

Unexpected Departure

Unexpected Beginnings & Endings

Unexpected Days

Eternal Port Valley: The Complete Collection

STANDALONES

Electric Love

Butterflies in Paris

All's Fair in Love & Vegas

Fumbling into You

Doll Face

Poolside Love

BEHIND THE SCENES

(each book can be read as a standalone)

Eras of Us

Not My Fault

Bad at Love

EVERGREEN VALLEY HOLIDAYS

(each book can be read as a standalone)

Tangled Up In You

How the B*tch Stole Christmas

SAPPHIRE FALLS ORCHARD

(each book can be read as a standalone)

Sweater Weather

THE HOLIDAYS WITH YOU

(each book can be read as a standalone)

I Saw Mommy Kissing the Nanny

Lucky to be Yours

The Only Reason

Ugly Sweater Christmas

POETRY

For Always

Holding on to Nothing

Say it Everyday

Midnights in a Mustang

Five More Minutes

When Lust Was Enough

About the Author

Shannon O'Connor is a twenty something, bisexual, self published author of several poetry books and counting. She released her debut contemporary romance novel, *Electric Love* in 2021. O'Connor is continuously working on new poetry projects, book reviews, and more, while also diving into motherhood. When she's not reading or writing she can be found watching Disney movies with her son where they reside in New York. She is currently a full time mom and full time author.
She sometimes writes as S O'Connor for MF romances and as Shannon Renee for Polyam romances.

Heat. Heart. & HEA's.

Check out more work & updates on:
Facebook Group: https://www.facebook.com/groups/shanssquad

Website: https://shanoconnor.com

facebook.com/AuthorShanOConnor

instagram.com/authorshannonoconnor

bookbub.com/authors/shannon-o-connor

pinterest.com/Shannonoconnor1498

threads.com/@authorshannonoconnor

www.ingramcontent.com/pod-product-compliance
Lightning Source LLC
Chambersburg PA
CBHW060453300726
48975CB00008B/2499